Edgar & Ellen

High Wire

Edgar & Ellen

HIGH WIRE

by
CHARLES OGDEN

illustrations by
RICK CARTON

Simon and Schuster, London

Watch out for Edgar & Ellen in:

Rare Beasts
Tourist Trap
Under Town
Pet's Revenge

First published in Great Britain by Simon & Schuster UK Ltd, 2005
A Viacom company

Design by Star Farm Productions LLC
Text and illustrations copyright © by Star Farm Productions LLC, 2005

1 3 5 7 9 10 8 6 4 2

Simon & Schuster UK Ltd
Africa House
64–78 Kingsway
London WC2B 6AH

A CIP catalogue record for this book is available from the British Library

ISBN 0689875398

This book is a work of fiction. Names, characters, places and incidents are either a product of the author's imagination or are used fictitiously. Any resemblance to actual people living or dead, events or locales is entirely coincidental.

Typeset by M Rules
Printed and bound in Great Britain by
Mackays of Chatham plc

WWW.EDGARANDELLEN.COM

Here is my dedication—

'Twas brilliant, and the teeming droves
Did gyre and gimble on the web:
With whimsy did Joi's charting groves
Bring crowds that would not ebb.

Beware the scrambling shark, my friend,
Sharon's cunning has no match,
And on the Robyn-bird depend
If chaos hath unhatched.

One fray! One prey did Peter slay!
His legal blade pierced print so small.
Flantastic day! Callooh! Callay!
I chortled down the hall.

—Charles

Willkommen

Nod's Limbs, 1807

"Cursed dwelling! Let dawn see you nothing more than a heap of ashes!" With mad intensity, Pierre Knightleigh struck flint on steel, sending sparks raining on the towering mansion's front steps. "Burn, burn, burn, I say!"

"Steady, sir," said a manservant, standing patiently at the bottom of the steps. "Perhaps you might rest in the carriage and reconsider."

"Confound it, Robbins! Don't you see? They're all *dead*. It's the only way . . . the only way to rid myself of the curse. I *must* burn it!"

"Please reconsider, sir," said Robbins.

Pierre redoubled his efforts to set the steps alight, muttering all the while:

> *"Nod built himself a dank, grey house,*
> *Went mad as any a Bedlam mouse,*
> *Then disappeared, and there bestowed*
> *Upon me this most foul abode.*
> *Hee hee!"*

Robbins cleared his throat. "If I may say so, sir, your recent tragedies are what trouble you, not this house. Your father's disappearance——"

"*Never to be spoken of!*" barked Pierre. "Never! The citizens of Nod's Limbs have been told Thaddeus Knightleigh died in his sleep, and they believe it." He turned his burning eyes to his manservant.

> *"If you're smart, you'll think it, too,*
> *For mayors don't vanish — madmen do."*

Pierre paused in his ditty. "But Robbins, I am both mayor *and* madman! Ho ho! Will I vanish like the rest?"

"Allow me to suggest that keeping this secret is contributing to your condition, sir——"

"What condition? *Look out for the camels!*" shrieked Pierre, jumping to his feet and pointing at the clouds. Then he sighed. "No, it was only a flock of weasels."

Robbins did not flinch. "A relief, indeed, sir. But if I may be so bold, the house can't be blamed for your father's, ah, passing, nor your wife's death."

Pierre dropped the flint and buried his head in his hands. "O, sweet Agatha . . . first your mother," he paused, and his voice turned bitter, "then your father, the *great* Augustus Nod . . . but why you? Why so young?" He turned to his manservant. "She grew up here, Robbins. This is where the curse was wrought. She watched her father fall under the house's spell, toiling, toiling, naught but toiling, day and night. It must burn!"

"The house is innocent, sir."

"Ah, but the house *isn't* innocent." Pierre leaned in close and spoke almost below hearing. "There are things in the basement. Unnatural things. Deep below ground . . ."

Robbins' eyes grew wide despite himself, and Pierre began to sing again.

> "*Sighs and groans and piteous moans,*
> *What lies beneath the pebbles and stones?*"

"It's the secret, Robbins," he whispered. "The mystical ingredient Nod put in his famous candles."

"The Waxworks candles?" breathed Robbins. "Like the Nigh-Everlasting Candle? The Vigour-Vapoured Taper? The Flambeau of Felicity?"

"The same," said Pierre. "The candles that earned him mountains of gold – the very stuff that gave those candles their power was wrought by devilry in the bowels of this house."

Robbins took off his tri-cornered hat and waved cool air over his face. "But we are men of the 19th century, sir. You cannot mean that you believe in witchcraft?"

"*Boo-dilly, ba-dilly, tra-la-la-lilly*," Pierre burbled. "Just like the money, you know."

"I beg your pardon, sir?"

"My inheritance is tainted, too. Nod disappears, and his wealth passes to his daughter – but alas! She has died before her time, and I, her husband, receive the bounty. Nod lined his pockets through unholy acts, and those same riches now fill the Knightleigh coffers. Have we inherited Nod's curse with them, Robbins, have we?"

The front door of the house creaked, and both men jumped. A stranger stood in the doorway, as tall as Nod but, unlike the town founder, he had a pleasant, amused expression. He wore colourful Bavarian lederhosen and a traditional Tyrolean hat with a peacock feather tucked in the brim. He held what seemed to be an unpowdered wig with a hen's egg atop.

To the man's shock, the egg *blinked*.

"You vish to remove this curse?" asked the stranger in a thick German accent.

"Wh-who the devil are you?" asked Pierre Knightleigh.

"This house, you are right, is a heavy burden for those who vould own it. I can take such problems avay."

"Who are you?"

"I am a collector of very special properties. If you sell the house to me, you vill atone for the terrible things that have happened here."

"See, sir?" Robbins spoke hopefully. "No need for an inferno. No reason to create further scandal. Sell the house and be done with it."

Pierre remained silent for a long while, his eyes fixed on the strange foreigner. "To whom shall I sign the deed?"

The man gave a smile so wide and eerie that both Pierre and Robbins recoiled.

"My name," he said, "is Sigmund Heimertz."

1. Edgar's Brilliant Deduction

Light flickered over the vast underground laboratory and its ancient scientific equipment, barely illuminating the pale faces of two children dressed in striped footie pyjamas.

Ellen sat on the floor surrounded by stray pieces of paper and peered into a yellowed notebook. The markings on the page were unintelligible:

"How's it coming?" asked Ellen's twin brother, Edgar, who stood at one of the nearby tables fiddling with jars and beakers full of a flaky, waxy substance.

"You try translating chicken scratch," Ellen snapped. "There's a page that's been torn out. Given our luck, I bet that's the key to the code."

"You've got to keep at it," said Edgar. "Augustus Nod kept all his secrets in that journal. Secrets about the balm, and, more importantly, secrets about Pet. We can't let that one-eyed hairball get away with any more tricks."

"And the parts he wrote in code might give us answers — I know, I know. But I'm not sure Pet is what we need to be worried about." Ellen remembered their most recent encounter with the Nod's Limbs mayoral family, the Knightleighs. Judith Stainsworth-Knightleigh and her daughter, Stephanie, Ellen's arch-nemesis, had tried to commandeer the twins' home and redecorate it. The twins had only just succeeded in beating them back. "The Knightleighs are still smarting from the whomping we gave them when they tried to take over our house. Trust me, Brother, they'll be back."

"The only reason they got so close was because Pet nearly turned you against me. I don't want to take any chances. Sister, Pet might have killed Nod, and now it could be after us! We have to find out all we can about what Pet is, what it wants, and what its true connection to the balm is."

Ellen picked up a notebook filled with her own writing and opened it to the following list:

THINGS WE KNOW

1. *The lab was built by Nod — town founder, Waxworks tycoon and FULL-TIME LOON*

2. *Nod was harvesting stinky goop from some sort of "balm spring" (Where is this spring?)*

3. *Balm proved useful in Nod's candles — long-lasting; also, customers who burned them reported feelings of "wholesomeness"*

4. *PET LOVES BALM — allows it to move at warp speed, cause trouble (Note: keep Pet away from balm)*

5. *Pet's tears (once it has eaten the balm) turn people into zombies of niceness (I can confirm: This is horrible)*

6. *Only known antidote to Pet poison: Seeds of nepenthes sinestros plant (thank goodness for Morella)*

7. *Heimertz is crazy (never trust an accordion player)*

8. *Pet and Heimertz now allies (Sneaky, wicked hairball + insane caretaker = major trouble)*

9. *Edgar stinks*

Ellen sighed in frustration.

The twins had lived their entire lives in the decrepit, towering house built by Augustus Nod. Their parents had long since left on an around-the-world vacation from which they had never returned and, for a long time, their only fellow residents were Heimertz, their unpredictable, ever-silent groundskeeper, and Pet, the one-eyed hairball of a creature who, though once the twins' favourite plaything, now seemed intent on making their lives miserable. Recently they had also started living with the ghost of Augustus Nod – or, more accurately, the haunting mysteries he left behind when he vanished 200 years earlier. The one fact they had was that Pet, the very same fuzzball they currently lived with, had been alive in Nod's time, and their queries into Nod's journal had led them to believe that Pet was responsible for the death of Nod himself.

"How is the analysis of the balm coming?" asked Ellen.

"I've made a recent discovery, Sister." Edgar picked up a bottle labelled "VINEGAR" and poured it into one of the jars of flakes. Almost instantly, the flakes dissolved and the liquid split into two distinct substances, like oil and water mixed in a glass.

"Voila!" he said.

"Great," said Ellen. "What does it mean?"

"I . . . I don't know yet. Still, it's fascinating." Edgar picked up another jar of balm, the last on the table. "Water, sunlight, and extreme cold have no effect. I'm trying heat next." Edgar walked over to a device comprising two tightly-wound coils connected with wires and a switch. He flipped the switch, and one of the coils turned orange.

"Wait, I think I'm getting somewhere with the code," Ellen said. "'*Z-u-c-chinis . . . grow . . . warts . . . in . . . winter*.' Blast! That doesn't make any sense. This is impossible!" She hurled the book across the room and it hit Edgar in the knees. He stumbled, and a balm-filled beaker dropped from his hands onto the heating coil.

"Ellen! We don't have much of this left!" cried Edgar. He tried to pick off as much of the substance as he could, but it was already too hot to touch. "Come on! Help me!"

But the balm began to glow and swell, and the twins stood transfixed. Wisps of smoke curled from beneath it, and little popping bubbles on its surface released spiralling steam.

"Edgar . . . should we . . . take cover?"

BLA-BOOM!

The twins dropped to the ground and covered their heads as the table flew apart, its shards landing in flames throughout the laboratory. Almost immediately the chamber was filled with black smoke. Edgar grabbed his satchel of gadgets and the twins crawled through the wreckage towards the stone staircase that led up to their house. A piece of rock dislodged by the explosion plummeted from the ceiling, just missing Ellen's head.

Edgar could barely see the steps through the smoke. "Almost there," he urged.

Then, two mammoth boots came into view on the bottom step. The twins looked up at a large man in overalls, who bore a huge, toothy smile.

"Heimertz!" the twins cried, stepping back into the smoky lab. The caretaker clomped forward and, in the dancing light of the flames, the twins could see that he held aloft a giant pickaxe, and that a one-eyed hairball sat on his shoulder.

"Trapped," sputtered Edgar. "If the fire doesn't get us — *hack-hack-hack* — that smiling madman will."

"The sewers!" Ellen gasped. She and Edgar turned and struggled back on hands and knees through the smoke and burning debris. They made it to the edge of the lab, which was only part of a much larger cavern. Here the ceilings were higher and the smoke thinner, but the twins kept crawling. A series of smaller explosions signalled the last of the balm reacting to the fire.

They could hear the lumbering footsteps of the caretaker following behind them.

"The journal!" cried Ellen. "We've got to go back for it!"

"There's no time!" Edgar pulled his sister forward.

"But our house! The fire—" Ellen turned to go back and this time Edgar yanked her pigtails.

"Don't!" Edgar shouted. "With rock that thick, our house will be safe, but the lab —" Edgar winced, "— is gone."

As they spoke, the outline of their hulking caretaker emerged from the billows of smoke, and the twins stumbled away again. The fire faintly illuminated the rest of the cave, but a persistent blackness in the floor ahead of them betrayed the presence of a vast pit.

"Careful," warned Edgar, who had almost fallen in once. The twins had no idea how deep the pit was nor what might lurk at the bottom. A huge pile of dirt and rock next to the hole caught Ellen's attention.

"That's never been there before."

"Who cares? Heimertz is still after us!"

With his heavy footsteps spurring them onwards, the twins reached the other side of the cave and found the concealed door leading to the Nod's Limbs sewer system. Only once they were among the familiar dank passages did they stop to rest.

"I have concluded," panted Edgar, "that the balm is extremely flammable."

"Impressive display of deduction." Ellen sneered. "You *blew up* the lab. *And* the journal. We've lost the only clues that could have helped us find out what Pet is and what it wants. What are we supposed to do now?"

Edgar thought a moment. "We've scoured our house and the journal for anything about the balm, Nod, and Pet, but there is *one* place we haven't looked yet. A place we know Nod frequented. A place that's been deserted for years."

"The Waxworks! Of course," said Ellen. She glanced nervously over her shoulder for any sign of the axe-wielding caretaker. "But we'd better hurry – we don't have many options left."

The twins took a direct tunnel to the abandoned Nod's Limbs Waxworks, and as they ran they sang:

> *What path to follow now that fire*
> *Destroys the knowledge we desire?*
> *Oh let the stones above this pyre*
> *Keep the flames from rising higher!*
> *But there isn't time to lose*
> *Though we are battered, burnt, and bruised.*

Onward, then, to seek the clues
To Nod's demise and other truths.
Still looms that bleak uncertainty:
If Pet killed Nod, what hope have we?

Meanwhile, in the moonlight just outside town, a strange caravan was also heading for the Waxworks. Thirty garishly painted wagons, packed with scores of squawking, hooting, growling, and roaring beasts, rolled through the otherwise silent night. The people accompanying them were dressed in a motley of plaids, paisleys, and polka dots. Each bore the same wide grin.

Leading the caravan was an older gentleman pedalling a unicycle. He pointed up the road at the abandoned Waxworks in the distance, and those around him nodded. Another man covered in tattoos wrapped a note around the shaft of a crossbow bolt and fired it over the treetops.

The bolt landed in the twins' backyard, not far from the decrepit shed where Heimertz lived. The note unfurled:

"We are arrived. Send forth the ithune. – B"

2. Working in Wax

"There's nothing here, Sister," said Edgar. After a brisk trip through the sewer system, they had emerged in the old boiler room of Nod's Waxworks.

The twins had felt hopeful when they'd found an office door marked "A. Nod, Proprietor". Nod's office had been dubbed a "Site of Some Importance" by the Nod's Limbs Historical Society, and was left exactly as it had been in its day. But the 200-year-old books, inkwells, and sheaths of documents provided no new information about Pet, the balm, the spring, or Nod's demise.

"I was positive we'd find something," said Edgar. He slumped on a moth-eaten sofa.

"I want to know what Heimertz was going to do with that pickaxe," said Ellen. "Pet was on his shoulder – what if Pet wants to kill us like it killed Nod? That dastardly dust mop could be using Heimertz to do its dirty work."

"It is!" hissed Edgar, pointing out of the window, and Ellen looked over to see the giant caretaker striding across the grounds of the Waxworks with Pet still perched on his shoulder.

"Get down!" cried Ellen, dropping to the floor.

"How did they know we were here?" asked Edgar. He shivered. "Is Pet *psychic*?"

"Psychic or psycho, we need to hide *now*," said Ellen.

3. Smell the Greasepaint

On the factory floor outside Nod's office, the twins found a row of tall, empty wax vats. The sides were still crusted with hardened beeswax and, though it was far less cosy than the office, the twins spent the night inside one of these. They flinched at every creak and groan of the floorboards, but neither Heimertz nor Pet appeared. Not until the sun was well above the horizon did the twins dare leave the abandoned building.

But when they emerged, the word "abandoned" seemed a poor description indeed. The expansive acreage that surrounded the musty wax factory was now a village of brightly coloured tents, caravans, and carnival attractions. Some tents were painted with exotic scenes of rampaging gorillas or men riding wild tigers, and all bore bizarre enticements in ornate lettering:

TREMBLE! 'fore this Mountain of Humanity!
The COLOSSUS!

SEE! Cutlery HURLED at Lovely Ethel,
Her life ever a TEASPOON from tragedy
AT THE ARMS OF THE STEAM-DRIVEN SPOON-O-MATIC!

WITNESS! BORIS the Creature Teacher
and his Academy of AARDVARKS, ARMADILLOS,
and ANTEATERS: Beasts OBEY his Every Word!

BEHOLD! Phineas the Emotionless

Recount your Funniest Joke, your Saddest Tale:
His Face Will NOT BUDGE!

HEAR! THE DEMON TRIO
How can MERE accordion, snare, and tuba
SPAWN such devilish merriment?

Two juggling clowns, clad in matching suits of green-and-yellow polka dots, hurled objects back and forth. First it was bowling balls and pins, then kiwis and mangoes, then decorative toilet seats and rolls of toilet paper.

"Amazing," said Ellen, stepping closer and ignoring the danger of catching a zooming toilet seat in the face.

The jugglers switched to flaming torches and miniature fire extinguishers; to finish their act, they triggered the extinguishers, dousing the torches in mid-flight.

"The circus, Sister! The circus is here!" cried Edgar. "The perfect place to lie low for a while!"

Ellen pointed to a banner hanging above them:
"Or maybe the worst place of all."

WELCOME ONE AND ALL TO
THE HEIMERTZ FAMILY
SEVEN-RING CIRCUS SHOW
AND CARNIVAL

"Heimertz?" whispered Ellen.

She heard an *ooph* beside her, just as a lasso fell over her shoulders and cinched her tight. Before she could even turn her head, the rope yanked her to the ground, where her brother already lay bound.

4. Good Knightleigh to You

Across town, Mayor Knightleigh, his wife, Judith, and their children, Stephanie and Miles, were out for a morning stroll. Normally these walks were pleasant affairs, giving the Family Knightleigh a chance to bask in the quaint perfection of their town — and for the town to bask in *them*.

"Howdy, Mr Mayor!" called businessman Marvin Matterhorn from his passing car. "Isn't that Miles getting big?"

"The day is as lovely as your family, wouldn't you say?" cried shopkeeper Betty LaFete, on her morning round with her pot-bellied pig. "What pretty purple shoes, Stephanie!"

Though this glowing attention was what got Mayor Knightleigh out of bed in the morning, today he could barely muster a grunt in response. His mind was on other things.

"I can't believe they did this to me again!" he shouted to his wife. "That circus always just shows up, no warning, no thought to the destruction it brings. It could be five years between invasions, it could be twenty-five, you never know!"

"And they're *slobs*," said Judith Stainsworth-Knightleigh, "with no manners whatsoever. So appalling, with their sawdust and their filthy animals and their peanut shells *everywhere*. This will just encourage Mayor Blodgett's nasty gossip about Nod's Limbs."

The mayor cringed. "Why does that gasbag have to visit *this* weekend? Does he have so little to do in Smelterburg that he must meddle in my affairs as well?"

"I thought you invited him, Daddy," said Stephanie. "You wanted to show off the hotel."

"Er – yes, of course. Won't he be blown away when he sees my masterpiece!"

At this, the mayor looked up over the treetops at the rooftop of the Knightlorian Hotel, the crowning achievement of the mayor's drive to bring culture, sophistication, and tourists to Nod's Limbs. After many setbacks and surprises (mostly due to a duo of trouble-makers in footie pyjamas) the hotel was nearly ready for its grand opening. The mayor beamed at his creation.

"Then you didn't get the message yet, I take it," grumbled Judith.

"Message? What message?"

"When Mayor Blodgett called this morning to confirm his arrival, that incompetent intern, Bob, mentioned that the circus had arrived unexpectedly. Blodgett wants to see it."

"Confound that Bob!" The mayor's cheeks reddened. "What do I underpay these interns for anyway? Now I have to take Blodgett to the circus. That sideshow of shifty, unscrupulous, scheming—"

"Why is the circus making everyone so mad?" asked Miles, the youngest Knightleigh. "I don't understand someone being mad at a clown. Clowns are everyone's friends."

"Stop your clown babble, Miles," snapped Stephanie. She shoved her hands in the pockets of her lavender tweed coat. "We have enough problems without listening to your nonsense."

Stephanie, too, looked up to the treetops, for there was another rooftop directly next to the hotel. Whereas the hotel was unblemished and fresh, this second building was bleak and disturbing. This was the house where the twins lived, similar to the hotel only in basic size and shape. Where one sported Nod's Limbs flags that waved to all who passed, the other was crowned with a rail of menacing black spikes. Where petunia borders and flowerboxes brightened the one, rocky patches of weeds, cracked panes, and rotted shutters blighted the other. Where one basked in cheery colour, the other swallowed it.

Stephanie ground her teeth. This dreary stone behemoth was the reason the Knightlorian had yet to open its doors. When Judith had tried to redecorate the twins' house in a bid to publicize the hotel, Ellen had, amongst other things, brought down a chandelier, caused a flood, and wrapped Judith and Stephanie in wallpaper, all of it captured on national television. The humiliation still haunted Judith, and she turned a glowering eye toward her daughter, whom she blamed for Ellen's behaviour that fateful day.

"*We* have problems?" snorted Judith. "No, some of us *create* problems and the *rest* of us have to clean up after them."

Stephanie hung her head.

"That house will be ours," Judith declared. "And, once it's a Knightleigh property, we will raze it to the ground."

"The perfect parking lot for my hotel," boasted the mayor. "Convenient, expensive, and *valet only*."

"So nobody's mad at the clowns?" asked Miles.

"Circus, circus, circus!" the mayor groused. "Let me

give that ringmaster a talking to, then I'll—"

"Daddy, I know what to do," Stephanie said. "If we just check town records on land ownership—"

"You'll stay out of our way, young lady," said Judith. "Your father and I will figure out a plan to deal with that blight—" Judith stopped suddenly and grabbed her husband's arm. "The circus *does* have something that would be enormously useful to us, dear. Perhaps it has come at the right time after all . . ."

The mayor listened closely and the family proceeded, not noticing the cloaked figure with a wide, eerie smile standing in the shadows of the Black Tree Forest as they passed.

5. Highly Irregular

Edgar and Ellen found themselves bound and dangling upside down from trapeze hoops thirty feet above the centre ring of the big top. A boy in a cowboy hat gripped the lassos that held the twins aloft. Four other kids, all with the same, albeit smaller, Heimertz smile, stood around him.

"The punishment is the same for all trespassers," said a tall girl of about the twins' age. "The Hoist!"

"The Hoist!" cried the others.

These kids were nothing like the Nod's Limbsian children Edgar and Ellen were used to. All of them wore at least one article of clothing that was torn or dirty or too big or too small. Ellen had never seen kids as grubby as she and her brother before.

"There's only one reason you'd be sneaking around the circus before it opens: you're burglars!" the tall girl cried.

"We're not burglars, we're . . ." Ellen hesitated, ". . . talent scouts! We've come to check up on all the new talent in the area."

"Yeah right," the tall girl said. "Talent scouts who scout talent in their pyjamas. Burglars!"

"Burglars!" the other kids cheered in unison.

Ellen scowled; she was unaccustomed to people not believing her perfectly believable stories.

"We've been captured by Heimertzes!" hissed Edgar.

"Who knows what they'll do to us. We've got to get away," Ellen whispered back. "You're the great escape artist. Undo these knots."

"I'm working on it." Edgar had managed to wiggle his fingers free from the ropes and was methodically testing and loosening each knot. As he did so, he began to swing back and forth.

"Ha! No city slicker can escape knots tied by Heimertz hands!" said the cowboy.

"We'll see about that." Edgar swayed close enough to Ellen to grab the knot that bound her wrists — a Hangman's Triple Hitch, one of his specialities. With a few perfectly placed tugs, he freed his sister, and then himself.

As the ropes fell away, Ellen grabbed her hoop and pulled her legs through it so that she hung upside down by her knees. She rocked upside down while Edgar swung back the other way, grabbed the tent pole, and slid down to the ground like a fireman.

"Way to go, Gonzo," the tall girl said, tweaking the cowboy's ear.

"*Ouch*. That was my best knot!"

Ellen then swung upward, snatched the next ring with one hand and monkey-barred her way across the rings to a nearby platform, which was covered with a colourful tarp.

"It took me two years to learn those rings!" one of the boys said.

Using the tarp as a parachute, Ellen floated down and landed safely beside her smirking twin.

"Showoff," Edgar muttered.

"Wait 'til you see my next act," said Ellen, as she and

Edgar advanced towards the band of circus kids. The tall girl held up her hands.

"That was a remarkable escape," she said. "No one has ever beaten 'The Hoist' before. Most towns we visit have the most *boring* people, and we have to have a little fun with them just to keep from dying of the tedium."

Edgar and Ellen looked at each other.

"That sounds familiar," said Edgar.

"And who are you? The circus janitors?" asked Ellen.

"I am Imogen," the tall girl said with a graceful bow. "And we are the Midway Irregulars."

6. New Bonds

"Well, I am Ellen, she who will soon be rubbing your nose in the dirt," said Ellen, returning the bow, "and this is my brother, Edgar."

"Big talk from a little girl." Imogen grinned. "Please, allow me to introduce the rest of my crew: meet the master of mirth, the incomparable *Gonzalo*!"

"Pleased to make ya'll's acquaintance." The cowboy tipped his hat to Ellen. "Ma'am."

"Gonzalo is studying to be a clown. Right now he's in his 'Western' phase," said Imogen.

Next she pointed to a sinewy girl and boy. "There's no height too high nor tightrope too narrow for Mab and Merrik, the youngest members of the peerless Hei-Flyers." Merrik bowed and Mab curtseyed.

"Any man may tame a lion or wrestle a croc," continued the junior ringmaster. "But who can master the will of the wily insect? None, save the indomitable Phoebe, queen of the flant circus."

"Don't you mean flea circus?" asked Edgar.

"Flants," corrected Phoebe, a tiny girl with a cherubic face. "Flying ants. *Much* smarter than fleas, and harder workers, too. I'd take a flant to a flea any day."

"I'm partial to fire ants," said Edgar.

"Fire ants *are* a good breed," Phoebe said. "Sometimes they guest in my show."

Ellen seized Edgar's arm. "Don't get too friendly with the locals, Brother. Remember these are *Heimertzes.*"

"And what's wrong with Heimertzes?" asked Imogen.

"A Heimertz has tormented us our entire lives," said Ellen. "And lately he's gotten so dangerously *strange* we can't be sure what he'll do."

"Oh, you must be the kids who live in the Tower Mansion with Ronan."

"What's a ronin?" asked Edgar.

"*Ronan.* Ronan Heimertz. Don't you know his name?"

"I never even knew he had a first name," said Edgar.

"He's not famous for chitchat," said Imogen. "He used to be our human cannonball, but then he switched to the caretaker thing. We haven't seen him for years."

"Boy, is he in trouble," said Gonzalo.

Imogen kicked him. "Quiet."

"What trouble?" asked Ellen.

"That's family business," said Imogen. "We're not to discuss it with—"

"My grandnana says Ronan betrayed us," said Phoebe, despite Imogen's glare. "She says he's going to stand in judgement at the tribble."

"It's a *tribunal*, Phoebe," corrected Mab.

"Stand in judgement," Ellen said. "I like the sound of that."

7. Doomsday on the Midway

A head the size of a watermelon poked through the tent's entrance.

"HEY, KIDS," his voice boomed.

"Hey, Manny," the circus kids called back.

"This is Manny, also known as 'The Colossus'," said Imogen. "He's the largest person ever born in Belize."

"PLEASED TO MEET YOU." Manny held out a hand and Edgar shook his thumb.

"BENEDICT SAYS IT'S TIME TO OPEN THE MIDWAY. COME AND WELCOME OUR GUESTS."

"Right. We'll be there in a minute," said Imogen. Manny retreated and she turned to the twins. "Time for us to go to work."

She led the other young performers out of the tent, leaving the twins behind. Finally Edgar broke the silence.

"This is the best place ever!" he said.

The twins headed out onto the bustling midway, and they couldn't help but marvel:

> *So many sights — just look! There goes*
> *A woman with a three-holed nose,*
> *That man who's whistling with his toes,*
> *Taught toads the violin!*
> *They may have humps or hairy ears,*
> *But these strange folk feel like our peers —*
> *Who'd guess that after all these years*
> *It's here we'd find our kin.*

A woman on stilts strode by, smiling that familiar Heimertz smile, and a compass fell from her back pocket. Moments later a bald man covered in tattoos snatched it up, shrugged, and gulped it down. He rubbed his belly with satisfaction and headed due north.

"This town has never seen anything like *this*," said Ellen. "What will our sweet, sappy Nod's Limbsians say?"

"I guess we'll find out," said Edgar, pointing at the dozens of townspeople coming through the entrance gate. The pristine, starched shirts and freshly washed faces of the citizens of Nod's Limbs clashed drastically with the wild hues, baggy costumes, and greasepainted faces of the circus folk.

The Poshi family approached Bartleby's Dubious Dunk Tank, where a clown (presumably Bartleby) sat in the dunk seat. He bounced enthusiastically and honked a bicycle horn.

"What is he trying to say?" asked Mr Poshi.

"I think he wants you to throw the ball at the target," said little Timmy Poshi. "And then he'll fall in the water."

The clown honked his horn repeatedly and pointed to his nose.

Mrs Poshi's face went stark white. "Heavens no!"

"I wouldn't want you to get your costume wet!" shouted Mr Poshi.

Nearby citizens nodded in agreement, with mutters of "Safer that way," and "Best for the fabric." The clown groaned. So did Ellen.

"They just make me want to tear my hair out," she said. "Or theirs." She stomped over and punched the target. The clown and his costume plunged into the water.

"Sister," said Edgar, watching several townsfolk help the clown out of the tank and offer suggestions for laundering, "don't you feel like we *belong* here somehow? Wouldn't it be great if we could join up?"

"What? Leave everything?" asked Ellen. "Even our house?"

"It's a lone isle of salty mischief in this sad sea of sugar, Ellen. And with Pet's new vitality and Heimertz's increasingly weird behaviour, can we even call it *our* house any more?"

"It *would* be a chance for real adventure." Ellen paused as another clown rushed by, tossing spoonfuls of coconut pudding at the crowd. Then she laughed. "Nice daydream, Edgar. But we're not letting Pet and Heimertz chase us off that easily."

Edgar laughed, too, but softly.

A commotion down the midway drew their attention. Crowds of circus folk parted to make way for a large man in grungy overalls. It was Heimertz. *Their* Heimertz.

The twins froze. His gaze was as fixed as his smile, and he paid no heed to his long-lost relatives as he lumbered past.

Before the twins could dash away, a tall, jowly gentleman with white hair rolled up on a unicycle and blocked Heimertz's path. The unicyclist wore a bright green tuxedo with tails, a golden waistcoat, and a black ring-master's hat. The twins noticed that the man was not *riding* the unicycle – he *was* the unicycle. His right leg ended not in a foot, but a single wheel, which he pedalled with his left foot.

"Hail, Ronan! Well met!" the ringmaster man called out. "We've missed you. How have you fared?"

Heimertz made no response.

"Glad to hear it," the ringmaster continued. "And how do you find life here in Nod's Limbs?"

Still nothing from the caretaker.

"Ah, our Ronan," laughed the man. "I agree with you: heaven is under our feet as well as over our heads!"

A crowd had gathered around Heimertz and the ring-master. For a family reunited, their faces showed an uncommon sadness. The twins approached cautiously to get a better view.

"It is time to listen to old Uncle Benedict now, Ronan. The tribunal begins in mere hours," said the ringmaster, clapping a hand on Heimertz's back. "Fear not: it will be fair, and what was wronged will be righted."

Heimertz twitched under Benedict's touch, but the white-haired gentleman showed no concern.

"Now, now – save your argument for the tribunal," said Benedict. "Ormond is more than ready to state the case against you. Be prepared to respond, or it will go poorly for you. Good luck, nephew." He bowed slightly to Heimertz and the rest of the assembled crowd, then wheeled away toward the funhouse.

Heimertz watched Benedict go, the familiar smile still plastered across his face. But this belied a bubbling beneath: Heimertz stuck out his hand, grabbed a metal support pole from a pie vendor's kiosk and wrenched it free. The structure toppled and cream pies avalanched to the ground; Heimertz barely noticed. He held the ends of the pole and bent it in half as if it were no more than a liquorice stick. The crowd backed away, and Heimertz hurled the bent pole like a boomerang. It whizzed between the twins' heads and decapitated a scarecrow behind them.

Two striped blurs dived into opposite tents.

8. Don't Believe Your Eyes

Edgar found himself in a black tent painted with red stars and silver moons. It was dark inside save for a few tiny candles lit here and there, and Edgar felt blindly around, looking for a safe place to hide. When his eyes had adjusted to the darkness, he could make out strange shapes hanging from above – chains, shackles, a straitjacket.

"A torture chamber?" Edgar wondered.

A cluster of candles flickered in the gloom, yet their glow was odd. Edgar approached cautiously; something beyond the candles appeared blurry. He rubbed his eyes, and when he opened them again another person stood in front of him. Edgar jumped back, then realized that he was only looking at his reflection in a large mirror.

But the image in the mirror started to change. The candles stretched upward, and his reflection morphed, growing taller and darker. He did not take a step, but the reflection appeared to come nearer, almost as if it were moving right through the glass.

Edgar fell backwards as a man stepped out from the mirror.

"*Who dares trespass in my cell of secrets?*"

Edgar scrambled to his feet.

"How did you *do* that?" he gasped.

The man crossed the tent, a velvet cape billowing behind him, and sat down in an ornate wooden chair. His flowing black hair framed a handsome face, and his deep cerulean eyes peered out at Edgar, unblinking.

"I have no time for meddlesome tots."

But an unusual pair of handcuffs on the wall had caught Edgar's eye. They were not like the chained bracelets used by police, but rather a solid disc of metal with two holes in the centre.

"The Cuffs of Jestofer!" exclaimed Edgar. "I thought those were just legend."

The seated man raised one dark eyebrow.

"You've heard of Master Jestofer?" he asked. "It is not his cuffs that are legendary, but rather those rare few who can escape them. Observe."

The man handed the cuffs to Edgar to examine. When Edgar returned them, the man deftly twirled them on his fingers and around his back like a true showman. Then, with a grand swoop, he slipped his hands through the holes and had Edgar latch them behind his back. He worked the cuffs with swift movements Edgar could barely follow. Moments later the restraints clicked and fell to the ground. Edgar let out a gleeful hoot. The man rubbed his wrists.

"Impossible is my name," he said. "Ormond the

Impossible." And then, without waiting for applause for his miraculous escape, he deftly slipped the cuffs over Edgar's wrists. "And I do not take kindly to intruders."

"I bet I can escape these cuffs," said Edgar.

"Unlikely."

"Not for Edgar, Escapist Extraordinaire."

Ormond looked amused. "Try not to hurt yourself."

Edgar struggled madly as he ticked through his list of escape techniques.

"Flanguini Twist . . . no . . . the Usher's Handshake . . . that's not right . . . the Sow's Hoof? Big Swifty? Aha! The Glazebrook Knuckle-crack!"

The cuffs clicked and Edgar lifted his hands in victory. He grinned and took a bow.

Ormond tented his fingers. "You do have some skill, Master Edgar."

"What else have you escaped from?" Edgar asked.

Ormond waved his hand.

"What have I not? Water jugs, pickle jars, glass boxes, the dreaded Black Mamba Basket . . ." He smiled, and Edgar again saw the Heimertz family resemblance. He shuddered.

"I should really find my sister," Edgar said. "Heimertz . . . er . . . Ronan is out there, and—"

"Ronan? What do you know of my cousin?"

"He's the caretaker of our property," said Edgar, "and he's certifiably insane. He just tried to kill us on the midway!"

"You reside at the Tower Mansion?"

"Yes, my sister Ellen and I do."

"I see. Your concern is valid, Edgar. Ronan has always been, well, what you might call . . . unstable. You are right to fear him."

Edgar pointed to a large sack near Ormond's feet. "Is that your satchel of props? Can I see your collection?"

Ormond slid the bag under his chair with his foot.

"Only the most worthy talent may unlock such secrets." Ormond considered Edgar thoughtfully. "With practice, that could be *you*."

"Really? I could show you all my tricks! I could be your partner!"

"Intriguing," said Ormond. "You would be a natural *apprentice*."

"Or that," said Edgar.

"I must warn you, though," Ormond continued, "the path to such an end is dangerous."

"Whatever this path is, it can't be more dangerous than Heim— er – Ronan. Ellen and I can handle any task the circus requires."

Ormond closed his eyes and sank back in deep thought.

"Introduce me to your sister, Edgar."

9. A Decision and a Mission

Ellen met Edgar and Ormond out on the midway.

"Hey, Edgar. Where have you been?"

"Breaking out of the Cuffs of *Jestofer*!"

"Big deal," said Ellen. "Gonzalo skipped clown practice and we went to see Hector the Dissector's act. He dissects live insects, then sews them back together with a tiny needle and golden thread, and the insect flies away again, as good as new." She stopped and eyed the stranger standing behind her brother. "Who's that?"

"Ellen, this is Ormond." The escapologist nudged Edgar. "Ormond the *Impossible*. And he wants to meet you."

"Greetings, fair Ellen," cooed Ormond with a graceful bow. "Edgar has praised you highly."

"Do you begin every conversation with a lie?" Ellen frowned and pulled her brother aside by his arm.

"Isn't it great?" he said. "I'm going to be his apprentice!"

"You're *what*?"

"This is it, Sister. This is my calling. Yours, too, if you'd stop being so stubborn. Look at this place!"

"First of all, when were you going to discuss this with me?" snapped Ellen. "And second, why would you even have this discussion with a complete stranger?"

"This one is different. They're all different here — they're not Nod's Limbsians."

"True, they're Heimertzes."

Edgar shook free from his sister's grip. "Stop embarrassing me in front of my mentor."

"You're embarrassing *yourself*, Edgar. Look at you — you're drooling."

Edgar wiped his chin. "This is our chance, Ellen. The circus is everything we've dreamed about our whole lives."

"Your dream of working as a magician's pet monkey, maybe."

Edgar pressed on. "Didn't it feel great taking on the Irregulars, Ellen? And the way you parachuted down from that platform — you're a natural!"

Ellen considered his words.

"Yes . . . yes that was fun," she said. "But you can't honestly be taking this join-the-circus stuff seriously."

"Think about it, Ellen. In the past few months, we've

been under assault from the Knightleighs, Pet, and now Heimertz. They're closing in on us from all sides."

"We can beat them back. We always do," said Ellen.

"We do? Our Gadget Graveyard is gone — Knightleigh's dismantled the world's best junkyard, and for what? To build the world's ugliest hotel *right outside our window.* Stephanie herself uprooted your beloved Berenice. And don't forget that Pet has been alive for 200 years — we don't even know if it *can* be stopped. Staying in Nod's Limbs is a losing battle!"

"Edgar, we *can't* leave," said Ellen. "If we do, Stephanie Knightleigh wins!"

"Wins what?" snorted Edgar. "She gets to be reigning queen of this gooey gumdrop of a town — you call that winning? Ellen, if we're on a never-ending adventure with the circus . . . *we* win."

Ellen tugged a pigtail and peeked over at Ormond just as the illusionist levitated a few inches above the dusty ground.

"Come on, Ellen, give it a chance!" said Edgar. "Let's 'join' for two days and have our run of the whole carnival. I'll bet by tomorrow night you'll agree that our real home is here."

"And I'll bet that after two days of being a bootlick to that showboating stooge, you'll be over this fixation."

Edgar looked his sister square in the eyes. "You're on."

Ellen walked back to the illusionist, who touched back down to earth with a yawn. "We will join with you and your circus, Ormond. But I will not roll tarps and hammer tent stakes while my brother struts around under the bright lights. I want to be part of an act, too."

"Excuse me, Miss Ellen?"

"We're joining the circus, Ormond!" Edgar beamed. "When do I start performing?"

"Wait, wait, please," said Ormond. "My striped friends, you do not understand. Such a thing is more difficult than you think. One does not just join the circus. One must be *invited*."

Ellen frowned and her eyes turned to slits. "I knew it, Edgar. There's always a catch."

"Not a catch, dear Ellen – a tradition, a time-honoured test to separate true-blooded circus folk from pretenders who wouldn't last fifty leagues." Ormond raised his arms, and his cloak thrust the twins in shadow. "To be invited into the Heimertz family circus, you must first pass a test, a traditional ritual. It has been our way of determining the worth of recruits for untold years."

"What kind of test?" asked Edgar.

The man glanced side to side, then knelt and huddled with the twins.

"Against my better judgement I shall set you down this perilous path," he whispered. "But you must tell no one, not even the closest of friends."

"Ha! We don't have friends!"

"Very well. Hidden on the circus grounds are three amber gemstones, each with a fossilized insect embedded inside: a spider, a cricket, and a dragonfly. I can tell you where to search, but you must recover them yourselves. Should you find all three stones and return them to me, you will have proven your worth. Then you shall receive your invitation."

"Is that all?" asked Edgar.

"We can do that," said Ellen.

"Cockiness and cleverness are not one and the same," said Ormond. "Each task requires special fortitude of mind and body, and if you are caught, you will never be welcome here again. You must carry out these tasks in secrecy. None may know the mission that you have undertaken, and only I will be aware of your actions until the end, whether failure or success your outcome be."

Ellen pulled a pigtail and grinned at her brother. Edgar cracked his knuckles and nodded back.

"We're in," he said. "Where do we start?"

10. Into the Funhouse

"Smoke and mirrors, my poppets," Ormond warned the twins as the trio approached a brightly painted structure the width of three barns. "Nothing is as it seems in the circus. Remember that. I will tell you only that the first amber can be found . . . in there."

"The funhouse?" Ellen asked.

Ormond's velvet cloak swooshed, and with a wave of his hand, he was gone.

"The *funhouse*!" huffed a familiar voice behind the twins. "Madame Dahlia, this is official mayoral business. I have no time for frivolity."

The twins ducked out of sight as Mayor Knightleigh turned the corner, accompanied by Madame Dahlia, the Mistress of the Botanical Bestiary. Dahlia climbed onto the funhouse platform and into one of the tiny cars that carried passengers through the attraction. She gestured for the mayor to join her.

"You ask to see Benedict," said Dahlia. "I take you to Benedict. Get in."

The mayor grumbled as he wedged himself into the front seat, rocking the car back and forth on its tracks. Madame Dahlia tapped a lever on the platform and the car lurched towards a tunnel painted to look like a clown's mouth. Enormous teeth chomped down behind the car and the mayor and his guide were swallowed whole.

"What business would Knightleigh have with Benedict?" asked Edgar, as the twins hopped into the next car.

"I'm not sure." Ellen pulled the lever. "But let's stick our noses in it."

For a moment it looked as though they would crash into the wall of clown teeth, but at the last possible second the mouth gaped wide and consumed them both. The inside of a clown's mouth, they discovered, is a dark place indeed.

Then the funhouse sprang to life.

Dozens of painted gnomes leapt up from a forest of plastic ferns. Their eyes glowed red as they tottered on their mechanical feet. A chorus of tinny voices chanted through a loudspeaker:

> *"Cloves and custard, clotted cream*
> *Will you laugh or will you scream?*
> *Sausage casings, mincemeat pie*
> *We all must live before we die."*

The gnomes sank from sight just as a great pterodactyl swooped down from the ceiling and brushed the twins' heads.

"Fantastic!" cried Edgar.

"I suppose," said Ellen.

At a bend in the track, faces sprang from behind dark doors like midnight in a cuckoo clock factory – Attila the Hun, Vlad the Impaler, and Ivan the Terrible, each twisted in ghastly dread.

"Better?" asked Edgar.

"Slightly," said Ellen.

Next, the car trundled past a series of misshapen mirrors. Through waves and warps, the twins saw themselves four feet taller, ten years older, and at last, three hundred pounds heavier.

"Is this what it feels like to be Mayor Knightleigh?"

"No, I don't feel any dumber."

They rolled into a spacious hall where jets of water whizzed just overhead amid a dazzling show of colourful strobe lights. They caught sight of the car ahead of them and, despite the waterfall that cascaded over the tracks ahead, the twins could hear the voices of the mayor and his escort.

"This way!" called Madame Dahlia as she hopped out of the car and disappeared.

"Don't leave me here!" whined the mayor. He looked frantically from side to side, then, just before the car passed through the falls, he leapt out and vanished off the track.

"They jumped ship!" Ellen shouted over the roar of the falls. "But where did they go?" They saw nothing but blackness on either side of the car.

"Guess we'll find out!" hollered Edgar. "Tuck and roll!"

11. Heir Looming

Edgar and Ellen landed on hard ground. Not far away, they could hear the mayor's wailing.

"Kidnapping!" cried Knightleigh. "Mayornapping! Help!"

A grunt, a tumble, and then nothing.

The twins crawled towards a sliver of light that seemed to come from the floor — it was a trapdoor. Ellen peered down into a room below.

"What is it?" Edgar asked, jockeying for a view.

"Shh! A ramp. It slides down into a . . . a trophy room, I think."

Ellen inched the trapdoor wider. The room looked like a museum of circus history. A gilded caravan wheel hung above a stately oak desk, a stuffed ostrich in the corner stood frozen in mid-stride, and a collection of peculiar masquerade masks gazed down from the walls.

Edgar jabbed his sister and pointed at the desk, where sat something that seemingly had no business being there: a rickety birdcage containing a one-eyed lump of hair.

"*Pet!*" cried Edgar. "What's it doing *here*?"

Ellen elbowed him in the ribs. "Shh. You'll give us away."

In the far corner Mayor Knightleigh sat uncomfortably in a carved chair with feet that were zebra hooves at the back and lion paws at the front.

Benedict stood by a window that looked out upon a cranking collection of gears, cogs, and pulleys. The mechanisms whirled in a precise ballet and filled the room with a rhythmic hum. Here in the bowels of the funhouse, the man had a superior view of the machinery that ran it all.

Ellen noticed that Benedict's right leg was no longer a unicycle; now it was covered in white feathers and ended in a scaly chicken foot with four fierce talons.

"Peculiar," she murmured.

Benedict crossed to his desk and propped his chicken foot upon it.

"Oh! An itch. Just now. I can't quite reach it," he said. "I hate to impose, Mr Mayor, but would you scratch it for me?"

The mayor curled his lip in disgust. "If . . . you insist."

He reached out and tentatively placed a fingertip on

the underside of the foot, then began to scratch. Suddenly, the chicken leg shot from Benedict's body and smacked the mayor's chest, knocking him back into the animal chair, which squawked like a kookaburra.

"Spring-loaded chicken leg," chuckled Benedict. "My most recent invention."

The twins covered their mouths to keep from bleating with laughter as Benedict gleefully kicked his legs up in the air. The right one sported a glistening white peg from the knee down: the chicken leg and, presumably, the unicycle were just costumes Benedict could wear over the peg.

The ringmaster adjusted the artificial limb. It was carved of whalebone and inlaid with jewels and intricate swirls of pure silver. He tapped the peg's gold tip on the floor three times.

"Lost my leg on safari," he said sombrely. "Wild animal attack at dusk. Swarm of Conganese dung beetles. Very nasty – but I digress. What has it been, Mr Mayor? Twelve years?"

"Twelve years too soon, some would say," answered Mayor Knightleigh. "And once again, we had no warning of your arrival—"

"My apologies, sir. It must have slipped my mind to tell you we were coming. We have things to tend to in the area, as you may recall."

"As it happens, that's the very reason I'm here," said the mayor. "*Your* family business is affecting *my* family business. I want to purchase it."

At this Pet's eye popped open. It scrunched back in its cage as if cowering in fear. Benedict leaned over and whispered, "Don't worry, little one."

To the mayor he said, "It is a precious family heirloom, Mr Mayor. An extremely rare find. Sigmund Heimertz came across it centuries ago, and we have owned it right and proper ever since, as you well know. It isn't for sale."

"I can offer a tidy sum. Just tell me your price."

"It is clear you are a man of means, sir," Benedict said

flatly. "I can smell the wealth upon you from where I sit."

"Why, thank you," said the mayor.

"Alas, I cannot part with it."

Mayor Knightleigh eased into his salesman's voice. "I can reward you handsomely for something worth *nothing*. So much cash that you could retire from circus life altogether."

Every trace of playfulness disappeared from Benedict's eyes. "It's been a pleasure sharing this time with you, Mr Mayor. Dahlia!"

It was Ormond, however, who appeared in the door-way.

"Madame Dahlia had a botanical emergency," he explained. "I will see the mayor to the exit."

"I'm offering *cash,* Benedict!" the mayor exclaimed.

Benedict patted the mayor on the shoulder. "Save your breath for the rest of the funhouse – the best screams come from the gut!"

Benedict closed his office door slowly behind the mayor. He walked back to his desk and softly stroked Pet's hair through the cage. Then he stopped, sniffed the air, and gazed up at the hatch in the ceiling, just as the two eavesdroppers pulled away.

12. Up in Arms

"How on earth did Benedict capture Pet?" Edgar asked, as the twins entered the funhouse's Maze of Mirrors. They had abandoned the automated car and were scouring the building on foot.

"He didn't capture Pet," said Ellen. "Heimertz must have given it to him. Heimertz wasn't stalking us last night, he was coming to see his family."

"It's like Ormond said," replied Edgar excitedly. "The circus is more than what it seems. It's not just a normal travelling show — it has business with Pet. Though I can't imagine what that is."

"And why would Knightleigh want it?" asked Ellen.

"Benedict said Pet is very valuable," said Edgar, "and rare — *extremely* rare." He bumped into a mirror and rubbed his nose.

"So is the bubonic plague," Ellen said, tugging her brother in another direction. "Doesn't mean I want to buy it."

"We should ask Ormond. He'll know," said Edgar.

"Right. Because Ormond knows *everything*," Ellen sneered. "Right now we focus on finding the first amber."

The twins emerged into the final room in the funhouse,

where a dozen rubber squids hung limp as windsocks from the ceiling.

"We're close, Brother. I can feel it."

"Sister, I immobilized the gnomes because you were *certain* the amber was in one of their beards," said Edgar. "And I impaled poor Vlad with my gasket cutter because you were *positive* it was in his helmet. And *then*—"

As Edgar walked closer to the squids, the sea creatures began to spin like tops. Light bulbs that lined the length of each arm flashed on and off, and a flurry of rubber tentacles lashed out, striking the floor with blind fury.

Edgar took a *thunk* to the head. He scuttled backwards to escape as tentacles cracked and smacked on all sides of him. Once he was out of reach, the squids deflated and darkened again. But a moment before they did, the twins spied a small bauble glinting in the eye socket of the largest squid.

"The amber." Ellen rolled up her pyjama sleeves. "How do we reach it?"

Edgar cautiously waved a hand in front of the nearest tentacle and it snapped out at him like a whip.

"Motion activated?" asked Ellen.

"I don't think so." Edgar studied the control panel on the wall. "Heat sensors. This is a state-of-the-art funhouse, Sister. Looks like an old rattrap from the outside, but—"

"Can you disable it?" Ellen interrupted.

"Of course I can disable it. We just need to run back to the house so I can get that blowtorch—"

"Look, Edgar – the tracks!"

Edgar looked where Ellen pointed and saw that the chain that pulled the cars along was in motion.

"They're opening the ride," said Ellen. "We need to do this *now*."

Then Ellen began what Edgar knew to be his sister's most despised activity: she jumped up and down, clapping her hands over her head.

Jumping jacks.

"Why are you doing that hideous exercise?" asked Edgar.

"Quiet. Sit still," puffed Ellen between leaps. "Save your energy."

"*Why?*"

"I'm heating up, (*clap*) dummy. If I can take (*clap*) getting lassoed and hoisted (*clap*) I can take some eight-armed (*clap*) jelly sacks," she huffed. "You just (*clap*) think cold thoughts."

Edgar nodded. "You are very brave. And very stupid."

"RAAAAAAR!" Ellen charged the forest of tentacles.

BIFF! SOCK! BIFF! SLAP!

Ellen's body heat drew all the squid aggression, making her a living punch bag. She ducked some blows, absorbed others, and, when possible, punched back. She deflected one jabbing tentacle into the head of another squid, which split open and fizzled dead. But for every arm she defeated, seven more entered the fray.

Edgar crawled across the floor quickly – but not too quickly – thinking of icy ponds, chilly sewer tunnels and cold pea soup. He held his breath and wriggled until he found himself directly under the largest squid. Edgar hopped to his footies and jumped. His fingers just managed to pluck the golden amber embedded in the sea creature's head and he fell to the ground, gem in hand. In the middle of the amber was a petrified spider.

"Mission accomplished, Sister!"

Edgar scarcely had a chance to smile when a heat-seeking tentacle pummelled him with a powerful punch. He tumbled to the other side of the room, where Ellen stood waiting.

"I hate seafood," she said, tenderly patting a fresh lump on the back of her head.

13. Watchful Eyes

Edgar and Ellen danced down the midway towards the tent of Ormond the Impossible, Edgar clutching the spider amber. On their way they sang:

> *Mirrors, monsters — there amid*
> *The tentacles the amber hid,*
> *But a bunch of nasty squid*
> *Can't match our nimble skill.*
> *Yet there's more than meets the eye*
> *To spider, cricket, dragonfly—*
> *In Benedict's strange chamber lie*
> *Much bigger puzzles still.*

The twins' tune ended abruptly when they witnessed dozens of circus folk marching gravely towards a tent at the far end of the midway.

"Heimertz's tribunal," Edgar said.

"Of course," said Ellen. "With all this amber business, I'd completely forgotten about it. Let's go and see what they do to him!"

"But Ormond – the amber—" Edgar protested.

"Your precious Ormond is probably already there," said Ellen. "He's making the case against Heimertz. We'll give him the amber afterwards."

"Outsiders aren't allowed, remember? How do you suggest we sneak inside?"

"No need for sneaking. We're going to walk right through the front door."

Ellen ducked into a small tent painted with neon spirals and beckoned Edgar to follow.

Just then Stephanie Knightleigh emerged from behind a souvenir stand and watched the twins with disdain.

"What a surprise to find those two weirdos here," she muttered.

The sunny face of Bob the intern poked out from the Funnel Cake Hut.

"Miss Knightleigh!" Bob's smile was coated with powdered sugar. "What a surprise to find you here! This urgent letter arrived at the Town Hall, and I'm here, um, diligently looking for your father."

He fumbled with an overstuffed briefcase, dropping his funnel cake and two corn dogs into the dirt as he retrieved a letter from it.

"I noticed the Mayormobile on the circus grounds, but I can't seem to find him," he said, blowing dirt from a corn dog.

Stephanie noticed the red wax seal stamped with an "H" crest – the mark of the circus family. She snatched the letter from Bob's hand.

"Daddy is in a private meeting," Stephanie said, brushing sticky crumbs off the envelope. "I will make sure he gets this, seeing that you have more *important* things to do."

"Yes, thank you!" beamed Bob. "Rumour has it that the Heimertz pistachio ripple fudge cup can't be beaten! Good day to you, Miss Knightleigh." And with that the intern ran off towards the dozen or so snack huts lining the midway.

Stephanie broke the wax seal and read the letter:

"Mr Mayor, I know what you want from the circus clan. They will not give it to you, but I know how to get it. Meet me behind Hector the Dissector's tent tomorrow evening at seven."

"Daddy's got enough to worry about." Stephanie crumpled the letter and tossed it into the gaping mouth of a hippopotamus-shaped trashcan. "I'll handle this."

14. Judge and Fury

The twins emerged from the clown tent disguised in bright polka-dotted jumpsuits, matching blue wigs, red bulbous noses and big, floppy shoes. Ellen squirted the flower on her lapel in Edgar's face and piped triumphantly on a pink kazoo. Edgar wagged a rubber chicken at her.

"Don't make me use this."

Accessorized with bicycle horns, whoopee cushions and a jumbo foam sombrero, the twins inconspicuously filtered inside the tribunal tent behind a bearded woman in a furry top hat.

The painted signs outside the tent promised "Death-Defying Deeds of Daring Do!" and "Gallons of Giggles for the Gaggles!" but on the inside, no such pledges were fulfilled; the space had been converted into a sombre, makeshift courtroom. In the middle of the tent a single wooden chair sat on a circular platform. The crowd of circus performers murmured nervously from the stands.

"*Good souls of the big top!*" A powerful voice thundered. "*Silence, I beseech you!*"

Ormond strode through the parting crowd towards the front of the tent.

"Brothers and sisters, we have business most serious. One of our own kin faces a host of charges for crimes against the family and must now be judged for them. I will state the case against him, and he will stand before his relations to account for his actions. Though each of us may speak his or her mind – whether in support or in accusation – Benedict, as ever, is sole judge of his fate. Where is Ronan?"

All heads swivelled as the twins' caretaker lumbered through the open archway. He stomped to the centre of the tent and plopped down in the chair; the wooden legs bowed under his weight.

Ormond approached the bleachers. "Ladies and gentlemen of the Heimertz clan: as difficult as it may be, I ask that today you hear the truth regarding one Ronan Heimertz who, for these past twelve years, has guarded the Tower Mansion and the destiny of the Heimertz family."

"What does he mean 'guarded'?" whispered Ellen.

Ormond spun gracefully towards the defendant, whose forehead now glowed with perspiration under the spotlights.

"RONAN!" bellowed Ormond. "Our *brother*, our

friend. For over a decade you have held post as sentry of valuable family property. For a time you faithfully fulfilled your sacred duties, operating within compliance of the charter set forth by the Heimertz High Council. You made sure the balm remained sealed away from those who would exploit it."

Edgar squeezed the rubber chicken and it let out a *toot*. A few family members cast disapproving glances his way.

"*Did he just say 'balm'?*" he whispered.

"*Did he just say 'family property'?*" Ellen replied.

Ormond went on. "As with each Heimertz before, you held true to the family code. But then . . ."

Ormond walked slowly past the packed bleachers, running a long, thin finger along one of the bleacher rails. He cast a steely gaze over the crowd before turning again to Ronan.

"Betrayal!"

Anxious murmurs rippled through the tent.

"Betrayal most profound!" His voice escalated. "According to the letters you yourself have sent to us, you have brashly acted against family wishes – against the laws of our ancestors! And despite the pleas and warnings of Benedict, you continue to disobey!"

Benedict, who sat silently off to the side, seemed unmoved as Ronan's bulky frame shook with boiled-over aggression.

Ormond continued. "You know the disasters that you risk in your heedless effort to unseal the spring, yet still you revolt! We have heard your excuses, and they are feeble. The truth is, you seek to profit from it! You have fallen victim to its corruption! You have turned . . . *traitor!*"

Heimertz rose to his feet, his chest heaving in anger, sweat dripping from his brow. His powerful hands curled into fists the size of cannonballs. Even his family members looked frightened.

"Benedict," said Ormond, pointing at the menacing

caretaker. "He's gone mad. You must banish him from the family!"

"Enough!" Benedict shouted with the voice of a man accustomed to commanding the centre ring. The white-haired man limped across the dirt floor on his whalebone peg, stopping between Ronan and the crowd.

"Calm yourself, Ormond. You have spoken well, but banishment is not a punishment easily handed down. Who would guard the spring?"

"Anyone here, if you asked it of them. What guardian has Ronan proved? He would dig up the spring for his own evil purposes—"

Before Ormond could finish, Heimertz lifted the wooden chair above his head and smashed it on the ground with a blow so mighty, even the mimes shrieked. The furious caretaker shoved Ormond to the dirt as he stormed from the tent. Sobs and murmurs of disbelief echoed in his wake.

Benedict helped Ormond to his feet.

"Now do you see, Uncle? He has become unhinged."

"You would do well not to aggravate him further." Benedict placed a hand on Ormond's shoulder. "Let me handle Ronan."

Benedict turned to the crowd. "This tribunal is now adjourned. Don't be troubled by the anger you see here.

Ronan has ever been our friend and thus has earned a moment's patience. We will revisit these matters when our kinsman has calmed, and we can draw from him a proper accounting of his reasons."

With that, Benedict tramped out of the tent, followed by the rest of the stunned circus family.

15. Special Delivery

Edgar pulled the red ball from his nose and approached the escape artist as the last of the family dispersed.

"Ormond!"

"Edgar. Ellen." Ormond looked nervously around him but the tent was vacant. "You should not have come here. The tribunal is not for outside eyes."

"We won't be outside eyes for long." Edgar grinned and held out his palm. The amber gleamed. Ormond's eyes gleamed brighter.

"Not much of a challenge," Edgar said proudly.

Ormond plucked the prize from the boy's hand and laughed. "Well done, my lovelies!" He rolled the amber between his fingers. "Did anyone see you?"

"No, but *we* saw someone."

"Benedict?" Ormond asked.

"And Mayor Knightleigh," added Edgar. "And you!"

"You saw the meeting?" With a sleight-of-hand trick, the amber disappeared.

"Knightleigh was desperate to buy something from Benedict," Edgar said. "Pet, we think."

"A pet?" Ormond looked surprised. "Benedict owns no pets, save that ridiculous stuffed ostrich—"

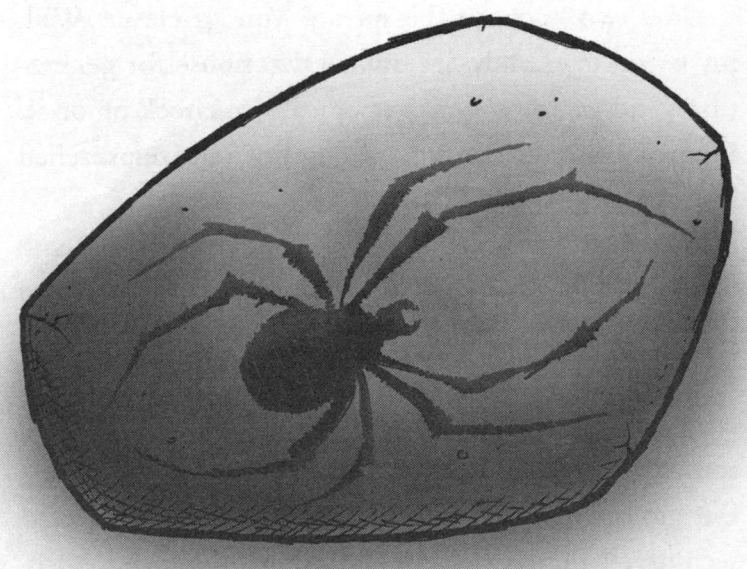

"No," Ellen corrected. "Not *a* pet. *Our* pet, Pet. That's its name. It was in Benedict's office, in a birdcage."

"Ah – the *ithune*," said Ormond. "It is the name my

family has given the creature. I can tell you only it is a beast of great value to my family. A beast Benedict wishes to keep safe."

"How does your family know about the balm and the spring?" asked Ellen. "And what's this about *our* house being *your* property?"

Ormond raised an eyebrow.

"You two know of the spring? You *are* clever. Well, my twins, my family has owned that house for generations, and we travel here periodically to check up on it. Ronan is only the latest in a long line of caretakers."

"Impossible!" said Ellen.

"Normally, yes, thank you, but not this time," said Ormond. "It is the reason for Ronan's trial. We guard the spring and the balm it produces. It is a dangerous substance, and Ronan's job *was* to ensure it stayed buried. Now, however . . ." Ormond trailed off, then turned back abruptly to the twins. "But that is a long story for another time. For now, busy yourself with the second challenge. You will find it is for the birds. Peacocks, actually."

16. Rube Awakening

A long line of Nod's Limbsians buzzed excitedly, waiting to get into a trailer topped with a giant, mechanical peacock dancing to the strains of a calliope.

"Esmerelda Vesuvius," Edgar read on the sign outside the door.

"Mistress of the Dancing Peacocks," finished Ellen. "This must be the home of the cricket amber." She frowned at the swarming citizens. "Too many people around."

"We'll wait until tonight, when everyone's at the big top show," said Edgar. "For now, let's enjoy our future stomping grounds."

On the midway, more townspeople guffawed at roving clowns, cheered for jugglers and stilt walkers, and gasped at sword-swallowers and fire-eaters.

"But that's so *dangerous*," said Buffy, proprietress of local bakery Buffy's Muffins, to the performers. "Wouldn't you rather swallow marshmallows and eat cream puffs? Providing you brushed your teeth afterwards, of course."

Edgar scowled.

"You don't suppose all towns we'll visit in the circus will be like Nod's Limbs, do you, Sister?"

"Other towns could never be as lily-livered as this," said Ellen.

They heard a sarcastic laugh behind them.

"Of course they can," said Imogen. "Just as timid—"

Gonzalo tipped his dusty cowboy hat and winked. "And just as gullible."

"You impressed us," said Mab.

"And that's not easy to do," added Merrik.

"Yeah," Imogen continued. "Never had a couple of rubes quite like you two before."

"Rubes?" asked Edgar.

"Simpletons. Yokels. Hayseeds," said Gonzalo. "You know – *townsfolk.*"

Imogen stepped to the front of the group. "We figured maybe you might have a trick or three up those pyjama sleeves. Something to make things on the midway a little more . . . interesting."

"*Now* you're speaking our language," said Ellen.

For the next few hours, Edgar and Ellen, with inspired assistance from the Midway Irregulars, caused more mischief and mayhem than they had since flooding the town with maple syrup.

Ellen and Imogen reopened the face-painting booth when Salvadora the artist left her post quite suddenly.

"Simple but effective," Ellen said, tucking the packet of itching powder back in her pyjamas.

"Sometimes simple is best," agreed Imogen as she

covered the booth's mirror with a black sheet.

Scores of Nod's Limbs children, wanting their faces painted like happy clowns or butterflies, skipped innocently away, transformed instead into zombies, ghouls, and the occasional vampire.

"Good idea to use waterproof paints, Ellen."

"Thank you, Imogen. Lovely wolfman on that last boy."

Across the midway, Mab and Merrik helped Edgar streamline and modify dozens of the elaborate blueprinted schemes he always kept buried in his satchel, and the results were spectacular. With minor tweaking, *Operation: Gullible's Travels* (which originally involved hundreds of plastic army men, mustard, and lengths of bungee cord) became *Moon Jump Mayhem*. Nod's Limbs children expecting a joyful bounce in the inflated playpen found themselves instead coated in yellow condiment with tiny plastic bayonet marks on their bottoms.

"Ellen and I always work as a duo," Edgar admitted. "We've never been part of a . . . a . . ." He fished for the word.

"A team?" finished Mab. "Merrik and I used to think the same thing."

"Prided ourselves on being a couple of loners," Merrik said. "But there's pranking power in numbers."

"I am beginning to see that," said Edgar.

"The circus will surprise you that way," said Mab. "We're like a country all to ourselves – our own laws, our own food, our own language, our own customs."

"Customs?" asked Edgar.

"Like never blowing your nose on a Wednesday," said Merrik. "Or tucking straw in your boot before you perform. Or lucky totems."

"Totems?"

"They're nothing fancy, just little things that bring you good fortune," said Mab. "Like Gonzalo. He has his lucky lasso. Imogen has a petrified lion's tooth. Merrik and I have a special trapeze bar – I carved it myself out of ebony when I was little. Merrik hollowed it out, and we used to hide little treasures inside. Kid's stuff, I know, but we're kind of superstitious about it. Do you have a totem, Edgar?"

"Hmm," said Edgar. "I like my collection of fire ants. I wish I had them with me now. They'd be perfect to unleash on The Squeamer ride."

Little Phoebe tugged Edgar's pyjama sleeve and offered him a rusty tin of breath mints. The lid was full of tiny holes.

Edgar gently shook the tin. "Your flants? What can they do?"

"I'll show you," said Phoebe. She took the tin back and opened it. A dozen winged ants buzzed upwards in front of Phoebe. She whispered a command and the flants fluttered into a pyramid formation.

Edgar watched delightedly as the flying insects zoomed in a tight flock toward Mayor Knightleigh, who stood near a concession stand with a bag of popcorn in one hand and a waffle cone in the other. In the blink of an eye, the flants knocked the cone to the ground and returned to Phoebe carrying the half-eaten bag of popcorn. The girl whispered to the flants again, and they turned the bag upside down onto Edgar's head.

Edgar beamed. "I have *got* to get some of those!"

"You can borrow them if you want," Phoebe said, blushing. "I trained them myself. We Heimertzes can talk to all kinds of animals. Boris the Creature Teacher works with armadillos, anteaters, rats . . ."

"Rats, eh?" said Edgar.

"Oh yes. And he helped me train my flants – they can fetch, roll over, play dead, even turn on lights and flush toilets. Just give them the command."

Meanwhile, Gonzalo attracted droves of children to the Milk Jug Melee with a rollicking display of lasso work on the biggest, softest, cutest teddy bear on the midway. Little did the contestants know that Ellen and

Imogen had glued the bottom jugs to the table, making it impossible for anyone to knock them down. Several kids were walking sadly away, vowing to practise their throwing, when an unmistakable voice pierced the din of the carnival.

"Well, look here," said Stephanie Knightleigh. "An escapee from the freak show."

"Beat it, Stephanie," Ellen seethed. "Before I stuff you in one of these milk jugs."

"Oh, but I want to play." Stephanie handed over a crisp dollar bill and confidently grabbed a ball. With a windmill whirl, Stephanie whizzed the softball at the pyramid of milk jugs. The ball hit the bottommost level dead centre and ricocheted back at her. The top jug wobbled and finally plopped over, but the other jugs remained unshaken.

"No *way!*" Stephanie roared.

"Ha!" Ellen laughed. "Nice fling, chicken wing. Thanks for playing. Next!"

"You're cheating!" Stephanie pointed a manicured finger at Ellen. "This game is fixed!"

"Sore loser," Ellen snipped, placing the lone fallen jug back in place. "Move along now."

"Oh, no," growled Stephanie. She snatched a bullhorn left by the absent booth barker. "You won't get away with this. Where's your treacherous twin? I bet he's in on this, too."

"You're going to eat that horn, Stephanie." Ellen took a step toward her nemesis when a strong hand clamped down on her shoulder. Madame Dahlia, keeper of the Botanical Bestiary, fixed Ellen with a fierce stare. But her expression softened as she turned to Stephanie.

"Ah, young miss," Madame Dahlia said. "Such loveliness you have to match great skill." She pulled the large bear from the top of the booth. "This is much difficult game – you deserve grand prize." She handed Stephanie the bear and casually retrieved the bullhorn.

"I don't *care* about the bear," Stephanie snapped. "My prize will be seeing this fraud arrested for robbery!"

"COME LOOK!" Madame Dahlia announced into the horn. "WE HAVE WINNER!"

Crowds of boys and girls swarmed Stephanie.

"You really *won*?"

"You're amazing – I tried three times and couldn't knock over *any*!"

"Of course I won," said Stephanie. "And yes, I am amazing, thank you. But they're *cheating*—" She was swept off by a flock of admirers who clamoured to pet her prize bear. After the tide carried Stephanie away, Madame Dahlia's grin became a stern frown.

"Um, thanks?" Ellen said.

"I am much disappointed in you, little girl," Madame

Dahlia said. She yanked the glued jugs from the tables. "We in Heimertz circus do not cheat. We play fair for all. Give me money you steal from good people and I find way to return."

Imogen and Gonzalo slinked towards the nearest shadow, but Madame Dahlia snapped her fingers loudly and the two kids froze.

"Imogen Deirdre Heimertz – Gonzalo Winston Heimertz!" Dahlia said. "I am more so disappointed in you who know better. Come to my tent and bring all your little friends. You wait for me and touch nothing."

"But—" started Gonzalo.

"Friends?" muttered Ellen. "Yeah . . . I guess they are."

"NOW," she said, towering over them.

Gonzalo winked and tossed Ellen his lucky lasso. "Best hang y'self now 'fore Madame Dahlia makes ya a snack for ol' Gustav."

"Who's goosed off?" asked Ellen, slinging the lasso over her shoulder.

"*Gustav*. A crazy plant big enough an' mean enough to swallow ya whole," said the cowboy.

"A big plant?" Ellen's pulse quickened. "That's something I've got to see. All right, *Winston*, let's go round up our friends."

17. Rara Flora

Imogen lit an oil lamp in Madame Dahlia's tent. Orange light spilled across canvas walls as Edgar, Ellen and the Irregulars funnelled inside.

A heavy arm flopped on to Ellen's shoulder.

"*Hii-yaa!*"

She spun and thwacked the cold appendage with her most ferocious karate chop. The limb was not human, however, but botanical. An enormous stem with a bulbous head the size of a medicine ball flailed about, along with a dozen other fleshy, green branches. The menacing flora hissed.

"*Nepenthes?*" Ellen gasped. "*Nepenthes leviathos?*"

"This here's Gustav. Told ya he was big," chuckled Gonzalo. The rest of the circus kids kept their distance.

Ellen, however, gazed in fascination. She loved her own *Nepenthes sinestros*, Morella, but she had never seen the legendary *leviathos*.

"Inflated petiole, double-hinged midrib," she said in awe. "Exceptionally large nectory zone with gobs of nasty digestive enzymes, no doubt. And those beautiful *teeth*—"

Ellen cautiously extended a bony finger toward the plant's open mouth. Suddenly the hood sprang open again, but this time a tongue-like tendril unfurled from the depths of the plant's craw and wrapped around one of Ellen's pigtails.

"Holy flapjacks!" exclaimed Gonzalo.

"Ellen!" hollered Imogen. "Get out of there!"

The tongue yanked Ellen to within inches of its mouth.

"Hey!" Ellen shouted. "Have some manners!"

Ellen punched Gustav's pulpy head, but the blows only irritated it, and the *leviathos* tugged harder.

"OUCH! LET GO!"

Dahlia entered the tent.

"Now why I shouldn't let Gustav swallow you whole? Hmm?" she asked.

"Because," Ellen grunted, "*Nepenthes leviathos* do not eat humans. Large insects, small birds, and the occasional wayward rodent. Have any voles? This poor guy is ravenous."

Ellen wrenched her hair free from the tongue.

"So, you know *leviathos*? Am impressed," said Dahlia.

"I have a *sinestros* at home," Ellen said proudly. "Her name is Morella. She has a wicked little bite herself."

Dahlia dumped a cup of dead crickets into the plant's mouth. It clamped shut, the stem receded, and the limbs relaxed.

"*Nepenthes sinestros*," said Dahlia with a faraway look. "A rare breed. None have been seen since before I join circus."

"Join? You're not a Heimertz?" asked Ellen.

Dahlia smiled an ordinary, reasonable, soft smile that in no way resembled the Heimertz family trait. "They adopt me in native country, a tiny girl whose parents die. From Heimertzes I learn to read, to write, and to clog in wooden shoe. They take me all over world to follow my calling: to collect plants no eye has seen." Dahlia dabbed her eye. "Miss Ellen, if you truly are owning *sinestros*, you will please to show me sometime."

"Show you?" stammered Ellen. "Okay. Sure. I'd . . . like that." She gave Gustav another pat and returned to the other kids. Edgar leaned over.

"What do you think about joining the circus *now*, Sister?" he whispered.

"I might be coming around to it, Brother," Ellen replied.

18. The Tale of the Mad Duke

Madame Dahlia picked up the lantern and led the children through red velvet curtains to her living quarters. She gestured toward a plush rug shaped like a rose, and the kids sat down.

Dahlia placed the lantern on a nightstand, and a baby

plant in a small pot next to it stretched away from the warm light, hissing softly. She sat on a splintery wooden bench and spoke not with anger but with solemnity.

"Tonight I catch you playing in way you think fun," she said. "But greed, sweet ones . . ."

"Dahlia—" Ellen said.

"Call her Madame Dahlia, Ellen," Imogen murmured.

"*Madame* Dahlia. It wasn't *really* greed. Just a little harmless scam. A game."

"No, young Miss . . ."

"Ellen."

"Miss Ellen," Dahlia said gravely. "You show greed, and greed is no game. It is dangerous. Let me tell you – centuries ago in deepest Bavaria, sick and ageing duke discover what greed is. He discover unusual spring – not with water, but with strange white gloop."

Edgar sucked in a breath. "A spring? With white gloop?"

"This old duke eat from bubbling spring, and it cure a shadow growing in his lung," Dahlia continued. "He use it next to put meat back on his bony flesh. His people watch amazed when duke get younger and have more strength than he have ever in whole of his life."

Edgar touched his sister's arm. "Ellen . . ." She nodded.

"Then," Dahlia continued, "he do what most man do with such treasure: he hoard for himself."

Imogen sat up. "I know what happened next, Madame Dahlia! The old duke rallied his fiercest warriors and raided tribal lands in search of more springs."

"He became a great and terrible warlord," blurted Merrik.

"Spreading death and misery across many lands," said Mab.

"But his obsession for more springs consumed him." Gonzalo had lost his cowboy accent. "The mad duke finally died, but legends of his Fountains of Youth spread like the plague."

Madame Dahlia nodded. "This is why Heimertz Circus travels world. We have found springs in every corner of planet, and is forever our duty to leave guardian at each. We protect from those who may come and abuse strange ointment — springs must bring no more madness to the world."

"Why do Heimertzes do this?" asked Edgar.

"Is family's curse." Dahlia rose to her feet and picked up her lantern. "Mad and greedy duke — he was a Heimertz."

19. Unseen Conspiracy

Stephanie waited behind Hector the Dissector's tent at 7 o'clock sharp. She checked her watch repeatedly: it was getting dark, and the show beneath the big top started at 7:30. The Knightleighs had seats of honour, and she didn't want to be late.

The bright lights and loud music of the grounds had faded as townsfolk and circus folk alike made their way to the main pavilion. Torches cast long shadows across the canvas tents.

She heard a soft footfall behind her, and whirled to see a cloaked figure peeking from behind the tent. She tried

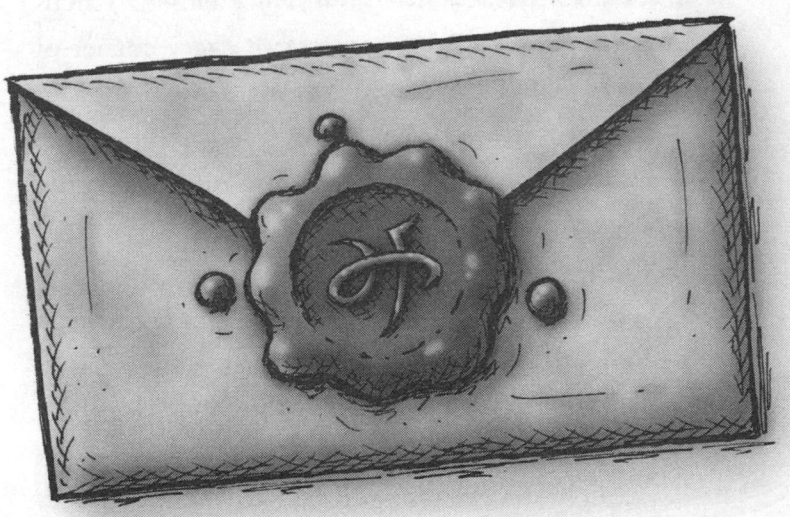

to peer into the hood, but could see nothing except a glint of white. Greasepaint, perhaps, or pearly teeth.

"Listen, I know you sent for my father," she said. "But it's just too risky for him to be lurking around here talking to hooded strangers. I'll handle all correspondence from now on. We will pay you handsomely if you can truly help us. Who are you?"

Without a word, the stranger handed an envelope to Stephanie, then backed away into the gloom.

Stephanie shivered. She ripped the envelope open and began to read.

> *"Everyone here is distrustful of me. I cannot move unnoticed, nor stop to talk, but if we work together we may achieve our common goals – yes, I know exactly what you want from Benedict. Follow these instructions precisely: first, you must take the one-eyed creature from Benedict's office in the funhouse—"*

"Stephie!"

Miles Knightleigh rounded the corner of the tent carrying a giant lollipop and a swashbuckling pirate hat he'd won at the ring toss.

"Ahoy, Stephie, we're going to be late," Miles yipped,

jumping up and down. "Clowns, clowns, clowns! Arrrrr!"

"I'm coming, Miles," she said, shoving the letter in her pocket. "Sheesh – no more sugar for you, okay?"

On their way to the big top, Stephanie swiped a last glance at the letter, then tossed it into one of the giant torches lining the midway. In moments it was ashes.

20. What Everyone Knows About Peahens

"I'm telling you, Ellen, this is the life for us," Edgar gushed as he and Ellen crept toward the peacock house. "Once we get these ambers, we'll have a lifetime of adventure ahead of us. New people, new places – a never-ending supply of *rubes!*"

Raucous cheers regularly erupted from the big top, but the darkened grounds outside it were empty. Edgar pulled his favourite lock pick from his satchel and approached the peacock house.

"Must you make *everything* difficult?" asked Ellen. She opened an unlocked window and dragged her brother in behind her.

Velvet cushions littered the floor of the peacock house. A gilt swing hung from the ceiling, and several cosy nests were tucked into nooks in the walls. A calliope organ was built into the far wall, and in the middle of the room a fountain filled the air with the sound of trickling water.

"They take care of their peacocks, I see," said Ellen.

"Judith nearly turned our ballroom into *this*," Edgar said. "It suits the birds better."

Ten peahens nested in the nooks, asleep and clucking peacefully. Ellen approached them.

"Maybe the amber is in one of the nests," she said. "Help me look."

"Careful," said Edgar. "The birds might be . . . danger-ous."

"Don't be a ninny, Edgar," said Ellen. "Everyone knows that peahens are very gentle. It's the peacocks you have to worry about."

"And where are *they*, exactly?"

"Not here, and that's all that matters. Now get over here and look in the nests while I hold the birds."

Ellen gingerly placed her arms around the first peahen and lifted it. But before Edgar could get a good look in the nest, the hen woke up. It cocked its head, examined Ellen, and started squawking and scratching like mad.

"Ouch! Ow-ouch!" Ellen yelped and tried to toss the peahen away, but its talons gripped her wrists.

The commotion woke the other sleeping birds. They

joined in the shrieking and stomping as Ellen and the hen bounded around the room.

"Quiet! Quiet, you stupid drumsticks!" Edgar yelled. Then he heard a low rumble like a sports car idling in low gear. He turned.

Three peacocks stood at the back of the room. With their tail feathers fanned out, they seemed bigger than beach umbrellas. The bird in the centre wore a golden band around its ankle marked "PAVO". They would have been quite beautiful, if not for the guttural thrumming in their throats and the menace in their golden eyes.

They charged.

21. An Invitation from Death

"The Spoon-o-Matic has hurled over 100,000 silvery ladles," called Lovely Ethel. "Its flexible arms throw thirty spoons a second with uncanny accuracy, coming within a cornflake's width of my body. Only three times has it missed – and we don't speak of those three brave Spoon Maidens who came before me. Can I escape their fate, or tonight will I become a victim of the fourth errant spoon?"

The giant target spun in a slow circle, and Lovely Ethel, strapped to its face, spun with it. She laughed as she whirled.

Across the ring from the target sat a chrome-plated machine with four drooping arms that grazed the floor like the branches of a weeping willow. But instead of leaves lining these branches, spoons protruded in neat rows.

Fearful murmurs rippled through the big top crowd, but Judith Stainsworth-Knightleigh crossed her arms and scowled. "I can't believe people are entertained by such unrefined behaviour."

Mayor Knightleigh, sitting next to his wife in the velvet-lined VIP box, nudged her with his right elbow – for on his left sat Mayor Blodgett from nearby Smelterburg. The visiting mayor clapped and cheered for Lovely Ethel just as heartily as he had for every act that had come before her.

"Shush, my sweetest," whispered Mayor Knightleigh to his wife, "Blodgett is enjoying himself. He's wishing that Smelterburg could attract such amusements, and I want to enjoy every minute of it!"

The arms of the Spoon-o-Matic began to curl and flail with a wildness more suited to a carnival ride than an accurate marksman. But with a series of whip-crack flings, the arms launched a hail of spoons at the spinning target – one-by-one, they struck handle-deep with a shuddering *thunk*, tracing a precise outline of laughing Ethel. Mayor

Blodgett, as narrow as Mayor Knightleigh was wide, leapt to his feet, hooting with approval.

"By golly, Knightleigh!" he said, smoothing his trim moustache. "I've never seen anything like it. I thought for sure this event would be another one of those public flops you're famous for."

"You beg my pardon!" protested Mayor Knightleigh.

Mayor Blodgett's smile faded slightly. "Easy, Knightleigh. Nod's Limbs has a winner. *This* time."

Mayor Knightleigh beamed. "Nod's Limbs will have a lobby full of winners, Blodgett," he said. "When my hotel opens, it's going to be the envy of every town for miles. Believe me, I'm putting Nod's Limbs on the map – er, I know we're already on the map, strictly speaking, but now our name will be in *big, bold letters*!"

Judith whispered in her husband's ear again. "This boorish rival of yours has seen the circus, and it's all been a success. Now please tell me we're not returning tomorrow night."

"Of course, cupcake. Tomorrow, we'll show him the nighttime view from the roof of the Knightlorian. If he's jealous of me *now* . . ."

Stephanie Knightleigh, sitting on the other side of her mother, leaned in and gave her father a warm smile. "Don't worry, Daddy, Mayor Blodgett will never look down on Nod's Limbs again. Unless it's from the Knightlorian Deluxe Penthouse Suite."

"Quiet, Stephanie," said Judith. "Your father is entertaining."

Stephanie blinked hard and stood up. "Um, excuse me, I have to, ah, replenish my caramel corn. Um, I might be a while." She pushed past her brother and slipped out of the VIP stand.

Lovely Ethel's act ended, and all seven rings of the circus lit up. Each was painted a single colour – blue, purple, green, orange, indigo and white – with the biggest centre ring in cheerless black.

In the middle of this ring stood a tall, gaunt figure in silky red robes. When he looked up, the audience gasped, for the man's face seemed the very image of a mummified corpse. Though the face was withered to little more than a skull, two fierce eyes flashed from their sockets.

"Tonight, you have met those who would gaze into the eyes of Death and dare to scoff," cried the red phantom. "Oh, aye, Death will not be denied – Death will always have its victory! But not this night. For now, it seems, Death must be patient for its prey."

The frightening figure strode closer to the audience, many of whom leaned back with its every step. "I hasten to remind all you living, breathing creatures that tomorrow when you return – and, yes, you *will* return – the most audacious Death-cheaters of all will make their one and only appearance of this engagement. The Titans of the Tightrope . . . the Captains of the Clouds . . . the Heimertz Family Hei-Flyers take to the airborne apparatus tomorrow night! No net floats between these skylarks and the perilous earth below! Will Death be denied yet again?"

Benedict removed the skeletal mask, revealing his smiling face. "And now, it's my pleasure to present the next act of wonder . . ."

As Benedict spoke, Mayor Blodgett whistled softly in wonder. "Knightleigh, cancel those touring plans tomorrow night. We have a date with the Captain Cloud Death Cheater Titans!"

22. Plumed

"Abort! Abort!" Edgar shouted as the peacocks closed in on them. "Ellen, get out of there!"

Ellen swung at her attackers, the peahen still clutching her arm.

"I . . . can . . . take . . . these . . . overblown . . . chick-adees!"

But with the grace of ballerinas the peacocks deftly

avoided her every blow, and got in several of their own.

"YOW!"

Meanwhile, the big peacock, Pavo, cornered Edgar by the calliope. Closer and closer it came, snapping its blade-sharp beak.

Edgar stumbled and – with nowhere left to go – fell backwards against the calliope.

Squonk!

The frenzied birds ceased their squawking for a moment. Edgar opened one eye; the peacock before him seemed to be waiting for something. So did the birds that had been attacking Ellen.

Without taking his eyes from the peacock, Edgar pressed another key.

Fwoot!

The peacocks all took a step back, and then to the right.

"That's it, Edgar," murmured Ellen. "The music! Play something!"

Edgar hesitantly began to plunk out his favourite dirge, an original composition he called *It's Your Funeral*, but the ominous melody only angered the peacocks; one took a fierce swipe at Ellen.

"Not that! Play a song they like!"

Edgar pawed through a pile of sheet music atop the calliope, as the peacocks approached again: *Birds of Play, Plumage Roundelay, The Mighty Pleasant Pheasant* . . . all too complicated.

"I'm no good at sight reading! I play by ear!"

One of the peacocks caught hold of Ellen's pigtail.

"I won't *have* any ears if you don't hurry!"

With shaking fingers Edgar fumbled through the first few notes of a melancholy tune titled *The Ballad of Pavo and Pym.* Instantly, the peacocks bowed, and the peahens moved reverently to the edge of the room.

"Keep playing, Edgar. It's working!"

As Edgar's playing grew steadier and more confident, Pavo pirouetted, waltzed, and strutted in a choreography worthy of the finest ballroom. The others joined in a chorus line behind him, performing swoops and leaps in perfect step.

Edgar reached the end of the number and, as he sustained the last chord, Pavo bowed once again and spread his tail feathers in a most exquisite display. Hues of green, gold, and royal blue unfurled in a delicate fan as broad as angels' wings.

But Ellen had her eyes fixed on something else.

The centre of each feather featured the distinctive turquoise "eye" that makes peacock plumes so recognizable. But the eye of the middle plume shone not turquoise, but orange. It was the elusive cricket amber, woven into the feathers.

"An excellent performance," said Ellen, plucking the prize. "But Edgar, you need practice."

With that, the twins departed the peacock house, singing:

> *Mere orange stone? Just peek inside*
> *To catch a cricket petrified.*
> *Those dancing peacocks could not hide*
> *Such a dazzling jewel.*
> *Two ambers found, just one remains*
> *Somewhere among the circus trains,*
> *And soon we'll bid 'Auf Wiedersehen!'*
> *To this town's cream-puffed fools.*

23. Sneaker

The twins collapsed behind Barnstorm Bertha's Balloon Beasts Stand.

"I'm surprised I still have hair left," Ellen said, stroking a pigtail.

"We should get this amber to Orm— *hello?*" Edgar jabbed his sister in her bruised arm. "I have movement

at two o'clock. And you won't believe who it is."

A girl in lavender staggered from the darkened funhouse. Her tailored clothes looked like they had mopped the floor at Greasy Billy's Gas Station, and a spot on the back of her head appeared to be smoldering. She carried an old birdcage with a familiar one-eyed hairball inside.

"Stephanie," Ellen snarled.

"And Pet!" said Edgar. "Knightleigh did want it after all."

"Come on, let's follow her," said Ellen.

The twins tailed Stephanie out of the circus grounds, but she did not head east to Knightleigh Manor. Instead, she hurried south towards Ricketts Road.

"Where do you think she's going?" asked Edgar.

"Maybe she's returning Pet to us," Ellen snorted.

But Ellen was wrong by about forty feet. For though Stephanie travelled up the nameless lane to the towering mansion, she passed the front door and tiptoed towards the shed that sat amidst the weeds of their yard – the humble home of Heimertz.

"Criminy," said Edgar.

The twins ducked behind a pile of rotting logs and watched as Stephanie deposited the cage outside the shed, knocked once, and dashed back down the road, past the hiding twins.

Heimertz opened his door and smiled down at the cage. He glanced left and right into the empty night, then hauled the cage inside.

"I don't get it," said Ellen. "Knightleigh wants Pet, but Stephanie gives it to Heimertz."

"Let's see what he's doing."

Through a cracked and grimy window, the twins saw Heimertz sitting on a three-legged stool, holding Pet. The hairball slouched in the man's mighty paw like a deflating balloon, and its hazy eye blinked slowly.

Heimertz reached under his cot and pulled out a black bag.

"HECTOR THE DISSECTOR" was scrawled across it in peeling paint.

The twins' eyes widened and they gripped each other's hands. Heimertz rummaged in the bag and took out a pair of tongs that ended in a sharp, wicked pincer.

"He's going to dissect Pet!"

Heimertz clanged the tongs once and shoved them deep inside Pet's tangle of hair. He wiggled the tool like Edgar working a lock pick, and then—

"*AIEEEEEEEEEEEE!*"

Pet's scream knocked the twins onto their backsides. The shed door burst open and the hairball bounded out like a tumbleweed in a tornado, scrambled across the yard, and leapt through a broken pane of glass into Ellen's greenhouse.

"Madness!" cried Ellen.

The twins bolted after the creature. The last thing they saw before they slammed the greenhouse door was Heimertz standing outside his shed, gazing after them, clicking the tongs quietly and grinning.

24. Journey to the Centre

Edgar and Ellen retreated to their house and barricaded every ground-floor door with furniture, but Heimertz made no move to enter. They exhaled for what felt like the first time in an hour.

"I am completely confused," said Ellen. "Heimertz and Pet aren't allies at *all.*"

"He's out of control," said Edgar. "He's gone from threatening others to actually harming them."

"Enough of this!" cried Ellen. She threw open the basement door and stormed through it.

"What are you doing?" asked Edgar, following.

"All this mess started with one thing – a spring of smelly gloop," said Ellen. "Well, it's underneath our house, and I want to see it for myself."

"But we've already explored everything down there – ah! Except the pit! Of course."

"Remember that pile of dirt and rock we saw next to it? That's the mark of Heimertz. It's where he's been digging."

The twins passed through the opening in a sub-basement wine-cask (which had been a secret door until Pet and an army of rats had heaved the twins through feet-first, shattering it). At the foot of the stone staircase, Ellen cranked the electric generator, sending power to the smattering of light bulbs that had not been damaged in the fiery balm blast.

They walked deeper into the cavern, using a penlight of Edgar's to guide them. Next to the giant fissure they noticed the mound of fresh earth that rose a Heimertz-and-a-half high. Next to it lay a pickaxe, a shovel, a bucket tied to a rope, and a wobbly-looking pulley.

"Heimertz chisels out rock and dirt and hauls it up with the bucket. *Look* at all the work he's done – he must really want that balm."

"Just like Nod," said Ellen, leaning over the edge.

"Maybe that explains why Heimertz turned on Pet," said Edgar. "Remember those journal entries about Nod harvesting balm all the time, and Pet getting angry about it? Maybe now we know why Nod disappeared: the furball stopped him from stealing the balm."

"Yes! And now that Heimertz is crazy for balm, Pet doesn't want him turning into another Mad Duke." Ellen stomped her foot. "That *has* to be why they're warring." She slung the rope through the pulley and picked up the bucket. "Lower me."

"What? You want me to give you a bucket ride?" snapped Edgar. "How do *I* get down?"

"Climb, fly, jump – your choice," said Ellen, handing her brother the rope. "Just get me down there."

Edgar huffed as his sister hopped in the swinging bucket and the rope went taut. With trembling arms, he lowered his sister and muttered.

"Should . . . let . . . you go . . . you selfish . . ."

When deciding to be lowered by bucket into a seemingly bottomless hole, it is always wise to first inspect the rope on which so much of the plan depends. Any rope – even one used successfully again and again to haul overloaded buckets of rock – may, after a time, become frayed. And a frayed rope is a weak rope, and a weak rope is trouble.

Edgar and Ellen were now very much in trouble.

"Edgar, did you hear that sound?" called Ellen. "Like a muffled sort of *twang*?"

"Rope . . . breaking!" grunted Edgar. "Happy . . . landings!"

"Edgar, don't you dare let me fall!"

The rope snapped right where it met the pulley. Edgar managed an impressive leap toward it, and though his fingers managed to grip the trailing strands of the flyaway rope, he was woefully unprepared for the force of the falling bucket.

Edgar was yanked headfirst into the chasm after his screaming sister.

25. Rock Bottom

"*Cough . . . cough . . .* Cripes!" gasped Edgar, inhaling a mouthful of dirt. When at last he could feel his toes, he stood up and shone his penlight toward the sound of moaning. Ellen crawled out from under the bucket, shaking dirt clods from her hair.

"Didn't bring a ladder, did you, Brother?"

"This isn't funny, Ellen. I can't even see the top."

Edgar examined the walls of the pit and, in the dim light, he could see a rough tunnel had been dug into one wall, sloping about thirty feet away. Wooden beams held aloft the ceiling, but it was a precarious bit of engineering and, even now, dirt streamed periodically from all sides.

"Heimertz really has to burrow to reach the spring. Dangerous work," said Ellen, eyeing the tunnel warily.

"If Nod was driven, then Heimertz is just plain crazy," said Edgar. "Thousands of tons of earth could fall on him at any second. Or us."

"We need to get out of here," said Ellen. She attempted to scramble out of the pit like a squirrel, but a chunk of the wall gave way, and she fell to the ground. The earth seemed to shudder, and the wooden beams groaned.

"What are you doing?" Edgar cried. "You're going to bring the cavern down on top of us!"

"Well, what do you suggest, Escapist Extraordinaire?"

"This is all your fault anyway! You *had* to go exploring the deadly pit when we were *this* close to hopping a circus wagon out of here!" Edgar hurled the penlight in anger.

"Edgar, be quiet."

"Be quiet? *Be quiet?* Listen to you—"

"*Shhh.* Look." Ellen pointed. From where the penlight had fallen, its beam glinted off a smooth, white rock protruding from the ground. Only it didn't resemble a rock so much as the top of a skull.

26. Sticks and Stones and Ancient Bones

The twins knelt before the white object. While Edgar held the flashlight steady, Ellen pawed the dirt away, soon uncovering a human skull that looked up at the twins with empty eye sockets. Ellen continued to dig through debris, and they discovered a spine, rib cage, sternum, and all the other bones that make up a human skeleton, right down to the toes. Only tatters of clothes remained – a waistcoat, breeches, buckled shoes – and an ornate ring around one knucklebone.

"Who is this? A victim of Heimertz?" asked Ellen.

"The bones are clean, so it isn't recent. And look at

these old-timey clothes. I think our friend has lain in rest for a long time."

Edgar brushed away soil from a metal object near the skeletal hand. He couldn't identify it at first, but the more he worked, the more it took on a recognizable shape: an oil lantern, torn to pieces. Stamped on the bottom were barely legible words:

PROPERTY OF

NOD'S LIMBS WAXWORKS

Do Not Steal.

Edgar sucked in a breath. "The lantern – blown apart. And there's only one thing down here that could cause that powerful an explosion. *Balm!*"

"The old clothes, the Waxworks lantern . . ." said Ellen. "Edgar, what if this is Augustus Nod?"

"If it is, we've solved the oldest mystery in town!" said Edgar. "Nod was carrying a flame down to the spring. He got too close to some balm, and BOOM! He brought the world down on top of himself, never to be seen again."

Ellen sat cross-legged next to the skull, gazing into the eye sockets. "The same thing could happen to us if we don't get out of here soon," she said. "What are we going to do?"

Edgar was too preoccupied with the skeleton's ring to answer. He pulled at the half-buried fingers, but the ring wouldn't budge. Frustrated, he tugged harder; the ring suddenly came loose and Edgar tumbled backwards into a support beam, knocking it out of place.

The walls gave way. Cascading dirt began falling in sheets, collecting around the twins' ankles, then their knees. Dust and debris filled the pit, and the twins coughed and gasped for air.

"This is the end!" cried Ellen.

"A horrible way to go!" Edgar wailed, when something danced past his eye. He looked up to see the remaining rope dangling from above.

"Ellen! Ellen! Grab hold! We can pull ourselves up – hurry!"

Edgar grasped the lifeline and heaved himself upwards hand over hand, as if it were the rope climb in gym class. Ellen followed behind him, and the twins inched their way up the rope as the pit filled up below them.

"Who threw down the rope?" Ellen called.

"Ask questions later!" Edgar shouted back.

The edge of the pit came into sight, and the twins could see their saviour – a small ball of dark, matted hair topped with a hazy yellow eye.

Pet had saved the day.

27. Recovery

The twins heaved themselves over the lip of the crater and collapsed, panting and wheezing. Pet sat patiently, gazing from one to the other.

Finally, Ellen got up and looked at the creature she and her brother had spent so many years tormenting.

"Pet, you rescued us."

In response, Pet nodded its eye ever so slightly then limped off towards the laboratory. Its shuffle looked more awkward and painful than ever. When it had gone a few feet, it turned back to the twins as if waiting for them to follow.

The twins shook the dirt from their pyjamas and followed Pet to the remnants of the lab. Ellen cranked the generator again, and they could see Pet at the foot of the

steps. Ellen leaned in and whispered in her brother's ear.

"If Nod died by accident, then Pet didn't kill him. We've been wrong this whole time."

"I wish we could talk to it," said Edgar. "Why did it save us?"

"I don't like this feeling, Brother," said Ellen. "Pet, Heimertz, the circus, the balm, and now Stephanie Knightleigh – they're all connected. But how? It's like we're caught in the middle of some mysterious battle, and we don't even know who our enemies are!"

"But it's starting to unravel. We know how Nod died now. We know his own greed killed him."

"Mad Duke Disease."

"Right. And, more importantly, we know that Pet didn't do it."

Pet shifted and the twins heard a crumpling sound. It was sitting on top of a yellowed piece of paper with a frayed edge. Edgar cautiously lifted Pet and examined the sheet.

"Ellen! This is the missing diary page! It's the key to the code in the journal!"

The paper was covered with the strange symbols and pictographs that ran throughout Nod's journal, and their corresponding letters and words in English.

Edgar scanned the page with an awed look in his eyes. "The code . . . it wasn't *Nod's* writing, Ellen . . . it's—"

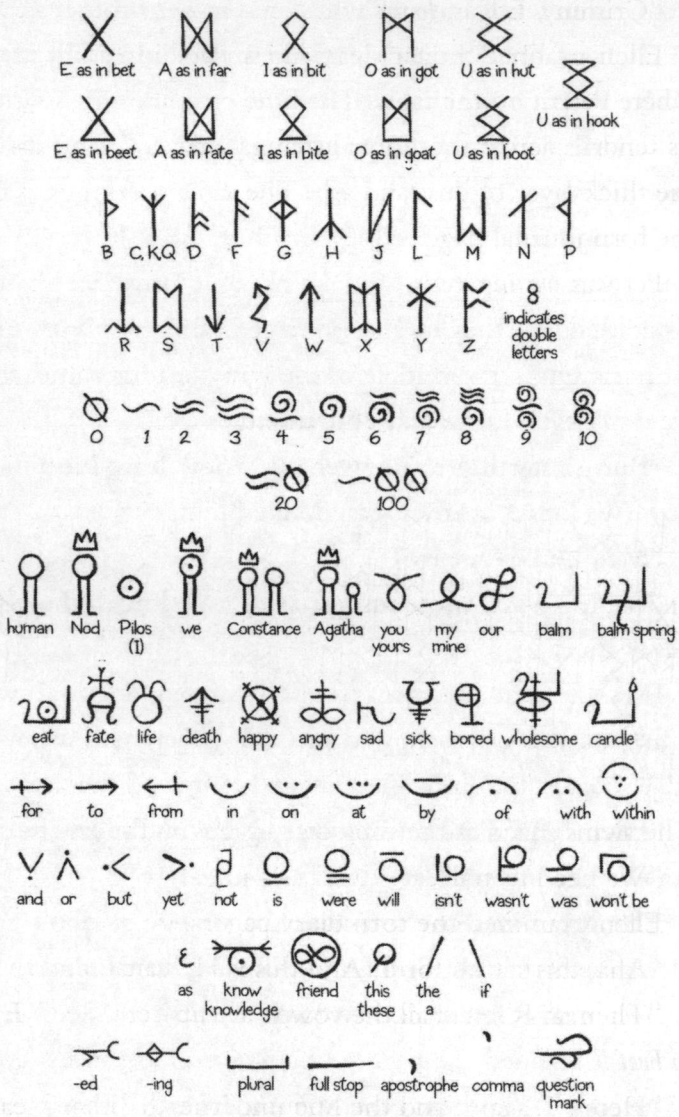

"Criminy, Edgar, *look!*"

Ellen grabbed Edgar's ear and swivelled his head to where Pet sat on the table. The little creature now swirled its tendrils across the floor, leaving intricate markings in the thick layer of dust and ash. The same markings as on the torn journal page.

Pet was *writing*.

28. Pet's Lament

The twins gazed at the elaborate glyphs and symbols.

"We need to translate this," said Edgar.

Ellen examined the torn diary page.

"Aha, this stands for T. And this is H," said Edgar.

"Then an R. And all the vowels are up here. See? '*E as in beet*'."

"Here's T again, and the line underneath. That means

a plural. So T–H–R–E–E–T–S," said Edgar. "Threets? What the heck is that?"

"No, wait – it was '*E as in bet*'. The first word is . . . threts. *Threats*? Your spelling is atrocious, Pet."

"The next word is S–U–R–O–W–N–D. No – that little symbol means double letter, so S–U–R–R–O–W–N–D. *Surround*. I see – in Pet's language, things are spelled like they sound."

Following Nod's key, the twins pieced together the rest of the writing:

> *Threats surround you as you perform these tasks,*
> *Yet, sadly, I can't answer all you ask.*
> *I only know another has foul ends,*
> *We must forget the past and live as friends.*
> *Beware, twins, what the caravans have brought,*
> *And give this thought.*

Pet stopped, exhausted.

"It's in so much pain," said Edgar. "Do you think it's because of what Heimertz did?"

"Of course it is," said Ellen. "Heimertz must be this 'other who has foul ends'."

"That means Pet's in as much danger from him as we are. Sister, I don't know why, but I think Pet's telling the truth – maybe it really does want to be friends."

"It did save our lives. We should return the favour."

The hairball resumed writing, its movements more agonized with every stroke.

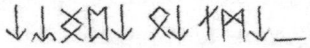

"That's the symbol for 'the'," said Ellen.

"S-E-R-K-U-S," Edgar translated. "Serkus. The Circus! Pet, we're already planning to leave with the circus. We'll take you with us! We're going to escape Ronan and this horrid little town."

"*If* we find that dragonfly amber," said Ellen.

"What do you mean *if*? We said we'd pass the test, and we will. We have to. I'll keep Pet in my satchel – we need to protect it from Heimertz." Edgar tucked Pet away and murmured, "Just one more amber and we're in."

The twins took their tired, aching bodies up to bed. But they both failed to notice the final line Pet had written in the dust:

29. Kept Secrets

On the way to the circus the following morning, Edgar practised sleight of hand with the cricket amber, making it disappear with a wave of his wrist, then pulling it from Ellen's nose.

"Knightleigh wants Pet," he said. "Why? And why would he have Stephanie deliver it to Heimertz's door?"

"It's confounding," said Ellen. "But I can't stop thinking about Pet's scream. It was horrible."

"It was the same when Morella bit it," said Edgar. He shuddered as he recalled the shriek when Ellen's carnivorous plant had bitten Pet some months earlier. "She clamped so hard, one of her toothy seeds broke off."

"Edgar, Morella only did what came naturally to her," said Ellen. "You're the one who *let* her bite Pet."

"That was an accident!" Edgar protested.

"Anyway, nothing good can come from a Heimertz-Knightleigh alliance. We must protect Pet – and ourselves."

They continued on, singing:

> *Our whole lives he took no care*
> *To weed the yard or fix the stair,*
> *But Heimertz partnered with the mayor?*

He's betrayed us all.
First this most unlikely teaming,
Then there came Pet's tortured screaming –
What's the purpose of their scheming
To harm the harmless hairball?

The twins arrived at the circus and went straight to Ormond's tent.

"Ormond!" Edgar shouted as the escapologist lay sleeping on a bed of nails.

Ormond woke with a start and sat up so quickly he pricked a thumb. *"Who dares trespass in my cell of –* oh, it's you two. How have you fared?"

"Once we join up, I know I'm not going to be working in the Peacock House," said Ellen.

"Yes, they're nasty stinkers," said Edgar. "But no match for us!" With a flourish, he produced the cricket amber from Ormond's nostril.

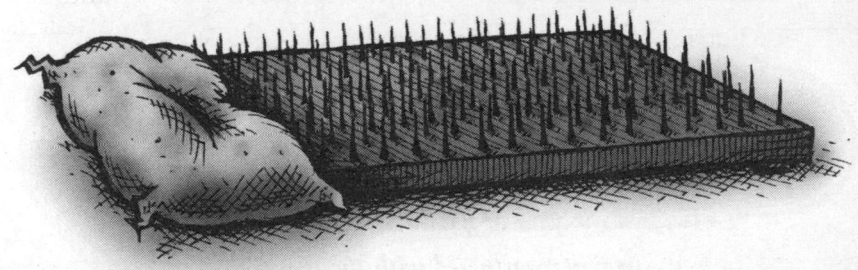

Ormond took the amber and smiled. "Perfection! You have superior peacock taming skills. Your sleight of hand, however, needs practice, Edgar." He pulled a cantaloupe from Edgar's armpit. "Now *that* is sleight of hand. There is but one amber remaining, then we may begin your training of such skills in earnest. Your final quarry resides in the House of Puppets, my poppets."

30. Plantastic

Edgar, Ellen and Pet (tucked safely in Edgar's satchel) took up a lookout position across from Pollyanna's House of Marionettes and Other Preposterous Puppets. They hid behind a rhinoceros-shaped garbage can until Pollyanna emerged, a short but sturdy woman whose arms seemed as thick as any strongman's. She locked the entrance and ambled away singing an off-key rendition of "I've Got the World on a String".

Edgar pulled a lock pick from his satchel. "We're clear."

"Move it, Brother." Ellen pushed her twin. "One more amber and we're on the caravan out of this town."

"Look who wants to join the circus now," said Edgar. "Guess I win that bet."

"Gloating doesn't become you."

Edgar picked the puppet house lock in seconds. He twirled his lock pick like a cowboy's revolver before slipping it back into his satchel.

"Gonzalo taught me that," he said.

Ellen bolted the door behind them and flipped a switch on the wall. A blue spotlight blazed on, illuminating a huge room filled with marionettes dangling from the rafters.

The twins pushed through the sea of suspended bodies. On stage, Pollyanna's puppets told the riveting tales of legends and heroes, but now, in the harsh light, they looked as lifeless as hanged corpses.

Twelve marionettes swayed beneath a banner titled "The Gods and Goddesses of Mount Olympus". At the front hung stern-faced Zeus, the king of all gods, holding his mighty lightning bolt and seemingly casting them a disapproving look.

"There's Hermes, the god of mischief-makers," said Ellen, pointing to a figure with winged sandals.

"Let's hope he's on our side," said Edgar.

Most of the marionettes were stranger creatures: centaurs and satyrs, gorgons and harpies, minotaurs, hydras, the Sphinx – ancient mythological creatures all.

"These are the best monsters from Greek mythology," said Edgar.

"And their habitats," said Ellen, pointing to hanging set pieces of landmarks and monuments both real and imaginary, like the Parthenon and the Gates of Hades. "The amber could be anywhere."

"I have a pretty good idea," said Edgar, looking up. The beam of the spotlight landed on a marionette dangling higher than the others in the centre of the room. A Cyclops, with a single, orangey eye.

"The Cyclops' eye. Of course!" said Ellen. "Not very hidden, though, is it?" She gazed up at the monster. "How are we going to get it down?"

"Leave that to me," said Edgar, and he pulled the tin that Phoebe had given him from his satchel. He opened it and the mass of flants gathered in front of him, awaiting instructions. Edgar pointed to the Cyclops' strings that were knotted to the rafters.

"Untie!" he commanded, and up and away flew the flants.

The insects disappeared among the rafters, and moments later the Cyclops plummeted to the ground at Edgar's feet.

"Too easy," he said, but before he could pluck the amber from the puppet's eye socket, the twins heard a clanking sound like the grinding of metal gears, and the Gates of Hades crashed down around Edgar as Ellen dived out of the way.

"A trap!" he exclaimed.

"Can you get out of it?" asked Ellen.

Edgar examined his prison: it was a four-walled cage with bars too narrow to squeeze through, but there was no ceiling to it. Edgar went to climb the bars.

"Ha, such snares are child's play to Edgar, Escapist Extraor— YAAAH!" The bars crackled as Edgar touched them and he leapt away. "This gate's electrified!" He rubbed his stinging hands.

"Electrified?" asked Ellen. "Who would go to the trouble?"

"You've got to cut the power source," said Edgar. "Hurry, before Pollyanna gets back!"

Ellen circled the cage on hands and knees.

"There aren't any cords attached, Edgar. I can't tell how it's getting power. There must be a switch or button somewhere that turns it off." She looked around frantically, but she could find no control panel among the craggy rocks and miniature skulls adorning the prison.

"*What fiend disturbs my puppets?*" a voice roared from outside. Pollyanna had returned. She jiggled the door handle, but the interior bolt held. "Ha! Mere locks cannot keep me from tearing you limb from limb, felon!" she bellowed.

"We're doomed," said Edgar. "Beaten by puppets. Oh, the shame."

Ellen flicked the light switches and pulled various plugs from their sockets, to no avail. She heard Pollyanna throwing her beefy shoulder against the door. Ellen grabbed a cluster of marionettes — two harpies, two gorgons, and a particularly clumsy hydra — and heaved them into the doorway.

Pet emerged from the satchel and, using a small jar of axle grease found inside, smeared a slimy pattern on the floor with its hair follicles.

"No time for small talk, Pet," Edgar said.

Despite the obvious pain the action caused the creature, Pet continued to write.

"Quickly! Translate it!" said Ellen.

"Now? Are you serious?" said Edgar.

"What else can you do from in there? Pet may have an idea, so *figure it out!*"

"All right, all right – I'll consult the key." He pulled the torn journal page from his satchel and worked out the translation in the dusty floor.

"Tib? No, no. 'Tis. 'Tis serkus ridl . . . no, two d's – riddl. 'Tis serkus riddl. Oh! 'Tis circus riddle! Okay . . ."

Boom! The door jamb started to give way.

"*Abandon all hope, thief!*" bawled Pollyanna. "Benedict warned me there was a rat among us! Is it you, Ronan?"

"Faster, Edgar!"

"Okay! I've got it! '*Tis circus riddle how to stop the volts – What's more electric than a lightning bolt?*'"

"Zeus' lightning bolt! Of course!" cried Ellen. She ran to the group of gods and yanked down the Zeus marionette.

"What is it – a hidden button? A lever?" Ellen tapped the tip of the shiny metal zigzag on the floor and drummed along the sides. "Anything yet?"

Edgar tested his bars with a finger but received a painful *zzzot*.

"Are you feeling the burn of Hades, evil-doer?" shouted Pollyanna. Her pounding began to make cracking sounds in the door.

"Aha, I've got it, Sister!" said Edgar. "The off-switch isn't *on* the lightning bolt – it *is* the lightning bolt."

He pointed frantically to a keyhole on the prison gates,

and Ellen jabbed the bolt inside. With a buzz and a click, the gates swung open. Edgar stuffed Pet back in his satchel as Pollyanna crashed through the door.

"I have you now, puppet bandit – GAAA!" The puppetress stumbled blindly into the mythological heap on the floor as Edgar and Ellen threw themselves through an emergency exit at the back. They hid behind a garbage can to catch their breaths.

"That was close," said Ellen. "I *thought* that amber was too easy to find."

"Did you notice what Pollyanna said? Benedict warned her. He knows our game." Edgar peeked inside his satchel and saw an exhausted Pet, its eye almost completely shut. "If it weren't for our hairy little ally . . ."

"Pollyanna was awfully worked up for this to be just a game, Brother. She was out for blood. I think the ambers are more than just trinkets. Ormond's not telling us everything."

"I'm sure he *has* his reasons. Besides, he has to answer our questions now." Edgar held the amber out. "We're in the circus family."

31. Key Information

The twins were just about to enter Ormond's tent when they overheard a muffled conversation. They peered in and saw Ormond sitting cross-legged in the centre while Benedict paced among the props. As he walked, his ornate peg — unadorned now by spring-loaded chicken legs or any other disguise — struck the ground with the sound of a gravedigger's shovel.

"Ormond, I wish you had consulted me before you sent a search party to Ronan's dwelling." Benedict stopped his pacing and looked at Ormond.

"You know my mind on this. I felt we needed to act the moment we heard the *ithune* was missing."

"It is unwise to make so rash an allegation." Benedict's eyes flashed and his voice betrayed a hint of anger.

"This is no idle accusation," said Ormond. He held up an empty iron birdcage. "Manny found this at Ronan's. But there was no sign of the man or the beast. Uncle, you must act or Ronan will hide the *ithune* where we shall never find it!"

"This is a grave discovery, to be sure," said Benedict, turning the cage over in his hands. "But before I make final judgement, we must hear from Ronan himself. It is our law."

"He had his chance. You and I both know he will not speak. The time for talk is over – you must banish him!"

"We must find him first," said Benedict. "I will speak to Dahlia. She and Ronan were close once. Perhaps he has brought her into his confidence again." The ringmaster strode purposefully out of the tent – step-*tack*, step-*tack*, step-*tack*. "Hold your eyes wide, Ormond. Mischief is afoot."

The twins emerged. Ormond hurriedly shut the tent flap behind Benedict.

"Ah, my little prowlers, it is a solemn day. Ronan has taken the *ithune* – it is in great danger, and still Benedict does nothing."

"It *was* in great danger," said Edgar, dramatically pulling Pet out of his satchel. "We rescued it last night."

"Why, I know not what to say! Quickly, put it away out of sight!" Ormond closed Edgar's satchel. "After all, we do not want word to get back to Ronan that you have the creature. His spies may be anywhere."

"Like in the puppet house? Someone set a trap for us. A dangerous one," said Ellen.

"Benedict suspects! Were you seen?" Ormond demanded.

"Ormond, you should have seen me," said Edgar. "Working quickly under pressure I—"

"Did Benedict *see* you?" Ormond interrupted.

"Nobody saw us," said Ellen. "Well, except for the puppets. But these ambers are clearly more than just a circus game. What are you not telling us?"

"The circus is a complicated society. Full of smoke and mirrors. What *seems* to be—"

"You've said that before," said Ellen. "But the only thing around here full of smoke is you. Why did Benedict try to trap us?"

"Children, don't you understand? Benedict is in league with Ronan!" Ormond gazed at the twins with wide eyes. "You witnessed the trial, did you not? You saw the crazed actions of your caretaker, his unbridled fury. He has defied family law by trying to dig up the spring, and now he endangers a defenceless creature – yet for all this, Benedict will not banish him, for he, too, has fallen victim to blind greed!"

"The Mad Duke . . ." Edgar said.

"Yes, it is my family's curse!" Ormond knelt down before the twins. "And it has wrought much pain and suffering, loss of life and . . . *limb*."

"Limb? Like a leg?" asked Ellen.

"I knew that beetle swarm story was bunk," said Edgar. "Now if it had been fire ants . . ."

"Benedict fell victim to greed once before and it cost

him dearly. I thought he had learned from his flirtation with treason." Ormond rose and shook his head. "It is time I told you the truth. What you play is no mere game; it is a quest of the greatest urgency. The ambers, Edgar and Ellen, are keys."

"Keys to what?" asked Ellen.

"To a secret safe. A safe that conceals the proof I need to expose Benedict and Ronan as conspirators. The proof *we* need to have them permanently expelled from the circus family."

"You could have just told us," Ellen said. "We want to bring Ronan down as much as you do."

"I feared the truth would be too much for ones so young. Had you known of the real risk—"

"We would have succeeded just the same," Edgar finished. He held out his hand and offered Ormond the final amber.

The escape artist gasped and snatched the orange gem. "Amazing! The two of you shall master the rings of the big top by my side when Benedict has been removed! Truly—"

And then Ormond froze. He held the amber to the candlelight and inspected it with a grim expression.

"We have been fooled," he said coldly. "This amber is no more than poorly cut glass. A fake."

"A fake? How can that be?"

"Clearly Benedict has outmanoeuvred us."

"The real amber must still be on the circus grounds somewhere," Edgar said. "We can still find it before the final show ends!"

"Yes, it is somewhere," agreed Ormond. "But Benedict will have hidden it well." He clamped a hand on each of the twins' shoulders. "I shall buy you time and offer what distraction I can. Swift be your footies."

Edgar and Ellen raced from the escape artist's tent as Pet recoiled into the deepest recess of Edgar's satchel and closed its eye.

32. Plan B

Stephanie sprawled across her purple bedspread reading her latest favourite book – *Bending Others to Your Will: A Beginner's Guide* – when she heard a single knock on her bedroom door.

"Enter!" she called. Nobody answered. Stephanie sighed and crossed to the door. "Miles, I told you – I will not be first mate to your Captain Scurvybeard. That stupid pirate hat does not make you the scourge of the high seas, okay?"

She threw open the door, but the hallway was empty save for another letter stamped in wax lying on the ground. Stephanie looked around suspiciously, but the mysterious messenger was gone, leaving only a faint aroma of buttered popcorn. Stephanie ripped open the seal of the letter and frowned when she read its contents.

> *"Stephanie – Good work, but the twins have interfered again! Still, we're going ahead with the second stage of the plan at the final show tonight. The instructions below may seem shocking. Even dangerous. But believe me, there is no other way for us both to get what we're after . . ."*

Stephanie shook her head as she read her conspirator's wishes.

"This is despicable! Just ruthless!" She tightened her lips. "And just the way to show Mother and Daddy what a great mayor I will be."

33. Uncloaked

The twins had little time before the final show, and they frantically scoured the circus grounds. The amber, however, was not inside the clown shoes, under the snake-charmer's baskets, or embedded in a bejewelled wagon wheel.

Tired and frustrated, the twins roamed the midway. Edgar held the fake amber up to the light.

"I can't believe Benedict fooled us," he said. "When you look close, you can see it's a crummy copy."

"If we don't find the real dragonfly by show's end," Ellen said, "I'll never get to cross-breed pigweed root with a *Nepenthes leviathos*—"

Ellen stopped.

"That's it!" she exclaimed. "Gustav!"

"Dahlia's plant? What about it?" asked Edgar.

"I can't think of a safer place to hide something than in its gullet."

"Killer squid, ninja peacocks, electrified puppet shows," Edgar said. "Giant man-eating plant? Makes perfect sense to me."

"Come on, we need to search Gustav before Dahlia moves her plants to the big top for the show."

The twins crept beneath a flap at the back of Madame Dahlia's tent. Gustav sat on a cart in the middle of a big room.

"If the amber is inside that leafy bear trap, how do we get it out?" Edgar asked.

Ellen snatched up a pickling jar full of bugs and twisted off the lid. "Leave it to me."

She patted the top of Gustav's head, and the plant snapped at her fingers.

"Easy there, big flora," said Ellen. "I'm not going to hurt you." She dangled a plump potato beetle in front of Gustav. "I just need to take a little peek—"

The twins heard a rustling as someone outside fumbled with the canvas door.

"Ellen, hide! Someone's coming!"

Ellen joined her brother behind a claw-leafed hibiscus tree. The tent flaps parted and a person in a dark, hooded cloak entered. The figure strode to the back of the tent to the sleeping quarters and lowered the hood: it was Madame Dahlia herself.

"I bring news," she said.

"Who is she talking to?" Edgar whispered.

"Her plants?" Ellen shrugged. "I talk to mine."

From where the twins hid, they could see straight into Dahlia's private room, where an outline of a large, lumbering man emerged from the shadows.

"That's no plant, Sister."

"Why would Heimertz hide here, Brother?"

"I come to warn you," Dahlia said. "Ormond find this in your home." From her cloak, she pulled the birdcage that had once housed Pet. "Only banishment will come if family can prove you stole *ithune*. Can you still dig out spring?"

Ronan Heimertz gently patted her back. Dahlia threw her arms around the twins' menacing caretaker and embraced him.

"Dahlia and Heimertz are – friends?" gasped Ellen.

"Looks like more than that to me," Edgar said.

"She's *helping* that lunatic!" Ellen was incredulous.

Edgar rolled the fake amber back and forth in his hands. "And you were worried about Ormond." But as Edgar spoke these last words, a clamour arose outside the tent. Startled, he dropped the stone and the fake gem rolled across the dirt floor.

Dahlia put her finger to her lips and motioned Heimertz to return to his hiding place.

"*Dahlia!*" cried a voice. "Dahlia, I must speak to you!" The twins immediately recognized the voice that had threatened them earlier that day.

Pollyanna of the Puppets marched into the tent. Several plants hissed and recoiled.

"Where is Ronan?" she demanded.

"Pollyanna, why you think I would know this?"

"Come now, Dahlia," said Pollyanna. "I know of your affection for Ronan, how it pained you to leave him those many years ago when he was selected to care for the spring."

"You know nothing," Dahlia answered coldly.

"You owe this family your loyalty."

"I *am* loyal. How dare—"

Pollyannna's eyes grew large. "What's this?" She bent down and picked up the fake amber from the ground.

"This stone was stolen from my puppet house this morning!" cried Pollyanna.

"I know not—"

"Liar! Ronan has been here! You are a traitor!"

The tendrils of one spiky plant thrashed wildly.

"Leave my tent."

"I'm going to find Ronan, Dahlia. And when I get my hands on that cretin, I'll show him less mercy than he showed my poor puppets. Then he'll be *banished*."

A bell rang out on the midway, and the twins could hear Gonzalo's crying, "*Come one, come all! The big top calls! It's time to baffle and enthral! Showtime! Showtime! Showtime!*"

"We must go to big top!" said Dahlia. "Show is starting!"

"We are not finished, Dahlia," Pollyanna muttered. "When I inform Benedict of this, you will be banished, too."

Gustav hissed and snapped at the puppeteer.

"You and your nasty little plants," Pollyanna added. She thrust the amber into Dahlia's hands. "Have a good show, Dahlia." With that, the puppet mistress left the tent.

Dahlia examined the fake amber as Heimertz joined her.

"I must go to show, Ronan. Stay here and think of next move for us."

The twins remained hidden as Dahlia solemnly collected the plants for the show on Gustav's cart and wheeled them off to the big top.

34. Snacks for Gustav

"I can't believe Dahlia is a traitor," said Ellen as she and Edgar joined the crowd heading to the big top. "Fine. I didn't want to teach her my botanical secrets anyway."

"We have bigger problems, Ellen. If you really think the amber is in Gustav, we've got to think of a way to get it out before the end of the show. Once we have the proof that Benedict is crooked, Ormond will take care of Ronan *and* Dahlia."

Packed inside the big top, the normally restrained folk of Nod's Limbs could not contain their zeal. Hoots and whistles filled the tent, as did calls to roving concessionaires who distributed hotdogs (with extra sauerkraut!), pretzels (with extra mustard!), and doughnuts (with extra sprinkles!).

The twins slunk beneath the crowded bleachers, propping the satchel on a pile of spilled popcorn to give Pet a better view.

"LADIES AND GENTLEMEN!"

Benedict's thundering voice echoed over the speakers and the crowd hushed. A single spotlight shone upon the ringmaster in his sparkling orange tuxedo. Tonight his right leg shimmered with red and yellow scales like those of a dragon. The peacock feathers in his tall hat bobbed softly, and his face bore the wide and mesmerizing grin only a Heimertz could muster.

"Tonight, you fortunate folk," he began, *"you shall witness a most magnificent cabaret of creatures, a profound play of performers. Behold, it begins!"*

At this, a band of ragtag clowns bounced, flipped and jumped into the spotlight. Some twirled long ribbons while others tossed handfuls of glitter into the air. The ringmaster was lost amidst the throng until he rose on a column of multi-coloured smoke. It seemed a magical storm.

"And now, I give you Madame Dahlia and her Botanical Bestiary!" The spotlight on Benedict winked out just as another to his left blinked on.

Dahlia's dress of emerald sequins shimmered like seawater, and her black hair, normally coiled into a tight bun, cascaded down her back. She uncrossed her arms and opened them to the ceiling like a blooming flower.

Before her lay a table loaded with spiky, knotty plants in black pots, standing at attention. In the shadows, just beyond the spotlight, sat Gustav, the towering *Nepenthes leviathos.*

"We're too late," cried Edgar.

"No, we're right on time," said Ellen. While the spotlight stayed tight on Dahlia, Ellen crawled toward Gustav.

Dahlia tossed a handful of bugs into the air. Writhing and rolling like charmed cobras, the plants snapped their jaws in choreographed savagery without letting a single insect fall.

"Eat, my beauties, eat!" cried Dahlia. The crowd murmured sounds of surprise and unease.

Ellen reached Gustav's side, rose to her knees and patted Gustav gently. The plant quivered.

"Easy, handsome," she cooed. "I just want to take a peek inside—"

Ellen got her wish. The plant unhinged its jaw, swooped down upon Ellen, and swallowed her whole.

Edgar let out a bleat. Pet, who had been peeking out of the satchel, ducked back inside. The plant settled on its fronds as if nothing had happened, just as the spotlight broadened to include it.

"Those of you with weak stomach may turn away now!" Dahlia boomed. "Gustav, world's mightiest plant and eater of many unsuspecting farm animal, is HUNGRY!"

Gustav's maw opened wide and juice trickled to the thick sawdust on the ground.

"So you think you like to eat ME, nasty Gustav?"

Dahlia yelled, moving closer to Gustav's reach. "You like to take bite from old Madame Dahlia, yes?"

The younger children in the crowd began to sob, and even some adults looked away.

Little Donald Bogginer couldn't contain himself. "Mommy, tell her not to do it!"

As Dahlia inched her head closer to Gustav, its jaws stretched wider and revealed row after row of vicious seed teeth.

"Madame Dahlia not afraid of overgrown vegetable like you! COME! I DARE YOU TO CHOMP ON MY NOGGIN!"

And in a flash nearly all of the woman's upper body disappeared inside Gustav's mouth. The jaws locked onto her midsection with an impressive crunch – in the crowd, the faint-of-heart screamed.

"Somebody save her!"

"Call the Fire Department!"

"She's too young to die!"

But before anyone could move, the massive plant released its mighty jaws and gently pulled away from Dahlia's body. The woman emerged unharmed – and in her arms she held the slimy form of Ellen.

"Look what I have found! Another victim!" Dahlia cried above the sound of resounding applause. But to

Ellen she whispered, "It seems *leviathos* eat people after all. And so playing with Gustav is very bad for little Ellen. Leave big boy plant to ones with true green thumb, eh?"

Ellen's mumbled retort was lost in the crowd's wild cheers. As the spotlights moved to the next act, she crawled back to her brother.

"No amber. And don't you *dare* say anything," she grumbled as she wiped off Gustav's slime.

"Oh, Ellen, did Gustav leave you with a bad taste in your mouth?" Edgar said, stifling a chuckle.

35. Flight of the Bumbling Bees

While Boris the Creature Teacher worked his magic with his army of armadillos, Edgar and Ellen ducked backstage. Their pyjamas and their pallor attracted little attention from the various costumed and painted performers.

"We've looked everywhere, Edgar." Ellen slumped against the Human Pinball's cannon. "*Where is that amber?*"

Then Edgar heard something. An older gentleman in a red-and-white striped unitard called out: "Children, brothers, sisters, cousins, ready yourselves! It is time for the Hei–Flyers to once again breathe rarefied air!"

"Hei–Flyers," mumbled Edgar.

The man stood among eleven identically striped Heimertzes of all ages. They stretched like cats and coated their hands with chalk. Mab and Merrik stood among them.

"Eureka!" cried Edgar. "The amber isn't *on* the circus grounds, Ellen. It's above them."

The twins tilted their heads back to see the trapeze bars hanging far, far above them at a height usually reserved for clouds and birds.

"You remember what Mab said about her lucky totem?" Edgar said. "Somewhere up there is an ebony trapeze bar that's hollow – it's our best shot."

Ellen nodded grimly. "Time to earn our circus stripes."

Moments later, Benedict announced "the world-famous Hei–Flyers," and the acrobats paraded out from the wings. They seemed to cartwheel straight up the five

great poles that held the tent aloft, and the crowd gave cries of astonishment.

Their leaders, Jens and Taryn, had been married by a young Benedict as they hung from swings above a beautiful waterfall, and they had not lost an ounce of skill after four decades in the centre ring. Performing now with nine equally talented relatives, they were legends in each town they visited.

Like a flock of pigeons, the Hei-Flyers filled the air. Their nimble bodies gracefully twirled and flipped across a series of platforms, tightropes, hoops, and trapezes that stretched the length of the tent.

Willem Heimertz landed on one of the platforms and quickly stepped aside so his younger cousin Katavina could join him.

But Katavina was nowhere in sight. The girl who did

step onto the platform wore a red–and–white striped costume, but hers was dirty and faded.

"Hello," said Ellen with a smile. "I'll be standing in for your partner this evening. Kindly step aside."

"Where's Kata?" asked Willem.

"*Mmph!*" said someone from inside a bag of juggling clubs fifty feet below.

Ellen grasped the trapeze, but its bar was made of oak.

Coming straight at her on the next bar was a very confused Anders Heimertz. Ellen grabbed one of his feet and climbed up his body like a squirrel. As they swung backwards, she inspected the bar, shook her head, and leapt away again. But she'd misjudged the distance to the next bar and fell.

Kristoph Heimertz, who swooped nearby on a set of hoops, grabbed the plummeting girl by the footie of her pyjamas, saving her from certain death. He deposited her safely on a nearby platform, right beside Mab and Merrik Heimertz.

"Ellen!" shouted Mab.

"What do you think you're doing up here?" yelled Merrik.

"Sorry, can't stay!" Ellen somersaulted past the siblings and flung herself towards a second set of trapezes.

Above them, Edgar moved along a crowded tightrope.

Instead of walking on it, he hung, swinging hand-over-hand beneath the feet of Jacinda and Eliza Heimertz, who yelped and wobbled precariously when they found themselves stepping on fingers.

The crowd cheered anew.

"These clowns are silly," laughed Miles Knightleigh from the mayoral VIP box. "And see? They're making everyone happy."

"Only two of them are clowns," said Stephanie Knightleigh. "This circus will let anyone perform."

Judith Stainsworth-Knightleigh peered disdainfully through platinum opera glasses. "These Heimertzes may know everything about high wires," she said, "but they know nothing about hygiene."

"How's it coming, Brother?" called Ellen as she soared by.

Edgar stood on the tightrope and balanced himself with a pole as he gazed down at the flying trapeze below.

"I don't see it yet," he cried. He took another step, but slipped. Luckily Kristoph Heimertz was sitting on a nearby trapeze, and he nabbed the end of Edgar's pole and swung him to the safety of a platform. The audience squealed.

Astride a tightrope on the other side of the tent, Jens Heimertz fumed. "Dirty birds on the wire."

"I'll wing these pigeons!" Taryn Heimertz barked as she leapt to a trapeze. She set her sights squarely on the strange girl quavering through the air like a poorly thrown dart. "Halt, imposter!"

Flipping and dipping, swinging and winging, Taryn and Ellen arced across the big top in a daring game of follow-the-leader. They travelled from one end of the tent to the other. Other members of the troupe tried to block Ellen's way, but the wiry girl wiggled out of every hand. Still, she could not find the ebony bar, and Taryn's clutches came closer and closer, brushing the ends of Ellen's pigtails and the trailing threads of her footies.

"Get out of our airspace, naughty children," huffed Taryn.

"This flight isn't over yet!" cried Edgar. Wobbling and pitching, he pedalled a unicycle with reckless speed on a tightrope that passed under the swinging pair. Despite his wild weaving, he managed to grab Taryn's toes and pull her down from the chase. The matriarch of the aerial crew suddenly found herself sitting unceremoniously upon Edgar's shoulders, careening madly on a bicycle built for one.

"They're going to fall!" shrieked Mrs Poshi.

"Darling, they only *look* dangerously incompetent," said

Mr Poshi. "That out-of-control acrobatic style takes years of training to master."

Adults and children alike laughed and clapped until their hands turned red.

At last, Ellen spotted a trapeze different from the rest. The ebony wood under her fingers was cool and polished – Mab and Merrik's lucky totem.

She alighted on a platform and unscrewed a cap on the end of the bar. A small yellow gem encasing a dragonfly tumbled into her palm.

While the crowd watched Taryn and Edgar untangle themselves from a pile-up on a platform, Ellen slid down a tent pole. Once free, Edgar leapt to the pillowy safety of an overstuffed candy floss cart. The twins scampered behind the bleachers to get Pet, still lying in Edgar's satchel.

"We did it, Pet!" Ellen exclaimed, holding the amber out for the creature to see. "We really did it!"

"All we have to do is get this to Ormond," said Edgar.

"Yes," said a voice behind them. It was the escapologist himself. Even in the shadow of the bleachers, they could see his smile. "All you have to do is give it to me."

Ormond held out his open hand, revealing the other two ambers, and he shook them together like dice. Ellen plopped the third in his palm and Ormond closed his fist quickly.

"Congratulations," Ormond said as he backed away. "You two have truly done the impossible." He bowed and smiled. "Now, if you will excuse me, it is time for my grand finale."

36. Wizard of Aahs

The circus orchestra piped a chipper tune to give the disoriented high wire crew time to clear the way for the next act. The twins flopped on their backs under the stands, and they sang exuberantly:

> *Success! Success! It's time at last*
> *To render Nod's Limbs to our past*
> *And join the circus' motley cast,*
> *'Midst acrobats and clowns.*
> *Ormond has proof that can convict —*
> *Ronan's cuffs have all but clicked —*
> *And the reign of Benedict*
> *Will soon come crashing down!*

"Let's go and choose which trailer we're going to call home," said Ellen.

"Not just yet," said Edgar. "There's one more act I want to see tonight."

The lights lowered, and Benedict's voice floated forth again: "*Mysteries from deep places. Enchantments from the dark unknown. Riddles from beyond our realm.*"

Another spotlight winked on, illuminating a velvet cocoon.

"Forget all you know of what's *plausible*!" Benedict thundered. "Cast off your notions of the *probable*! The evening now belongs to . . . the *Impossible*!"

The cocoon unfurled to reveal Ormond, and he flung off his velvet cloak. Two sequinned assistants swooped in to bind his body in a straitjacket, then in links of thick chains.

"Tighter!" Ormond exclaimed. "More chains! More locks!"

"He is a true master." Edgar shook his head with awe. "Those locks are genuine Stock Maidens!"

Once he was bound like a mummy, Ormond's assistants hooked a thin wire to his boots, and in moments he was suspended over an open steamer trunk.

As the cable lowered Ormond into the trunk, he craned his neck to address the audience.

"Where you see chains and straitjackets, I see only paperclips and windbreakers. Is this all that can be brought to challenge me?"

Just then Manny the Colossus emerged from the

shadows. Behind him he dragged a glass tank filled with a liquid too thick and dark to be water.

"What new devilry is this?" Ormond bellowed. "Do I smell maple syrup?"

"Syrup? Did he say syrup?" buzzed several in the audience. A shudder rippled around the tent – memories of the recent French Toast Festival disaster.

"Perhaps I have spoken too soon! Is the test not great enough without so perilously sweet a sepulchre?" Ormond shouted. "Surely no artist, no matter the pedigree, could escape such a cruel and sticky fate!"

"Don't do it!" cried Suzette Croquet.

"You'll never get that syrup out of your loafers!" called Wesley Puddlesby.

"Should I not emerge, dear friends," Ormond boomed, "remember me each time you dine on pancake!"

"Such dramatic flair," Edgar said. "I need to work on my flair."

Ormond disappeared into the trunk and his assistants fastened its many locks. Then Manny heaved the vessel into the syrup. The crowd fell silent, all eyes turned to the deathly pool. Several seconds passed and nothing emerged. Even Judith Stainsworth-Knightleigh began to fidget.

"Shouldn't you do something?" She poked her husband, who sat on the edge of his seat munching kettle corn.

"Hmm?"

"We cannot afford the bad press from a grisly death in our town," whispered Judith. She glanced at Mayor Blodgett, who was nervously chewing his fingernails. "Even if it's one of these . . . these carnival people."

"Well, dear," mumbled the mayor, taking a bite of the funnel cake in his other hand, "I am not so sure this falls under my jurisdiction—"

Stephanie Knightleigh spied the twins lurking near the bleachers.

"Always trying to ruin *everything*." She gazed down at the piece of paper crumpled in her hand, then she stood up and smoothed out her lavender dress. "Still, I suppose it's no worse than what I'm about to do."

With her family distracted by the dangerous escape act, Stephanie slipped out of the VIP box and headed for the outer ring where the Spoon-o-Matic waited. She crouched in the shadow of the mammoth machine, holding a rope that disappeared under a bleacher.

"Ten . . . nine . . . eight . . . seven . . ." She put a foot on the lever at the base of the Spoon-o-Matic. Meanwhile, the townspeople were starting to panic.

"Hurry!" yelled Eugenia Smithy.

"He's going to run out of air!" screamed Nancy Weedle.

"Six ... five ... four ..." Stephanie stepped hard on the lever. The machinery inside the Spoon-o-Matic hummed as it warmed up, but the crowd was too enthralled by Ormond's act to notice.

"Three ... two ..." Stephanie turned the dial on the

machine past "Friendly Toss" and "Hearty Hurl", all the way to the maximum position: "Fling Like Mad".

"One . . ." Stephanie took a deep breath. "This is for you, Mother," she said, and she pulled the rope hard. The other end yanked the firing pin on the Human Pinball's cannon. It clicked down and sparked.

The tense silence was broken by an unexpected – and most unpleasant – *KER-BOOOOOM!*

37. Top This

Instead of firing the Human Pinball through the air, the cannon launched a *real* cannonball. The big gun had been aimed at the pole that held up the middle of the tent; the ball struck the pole in the middle and fractured it with a sickening, splintering sound.

The giant mast was now dangerously close to snapping in two. The canvas ceiling flapped like a bed sheet in the wind. The surrounding poles leaned inward, and the web of ropes that held the tent aloft groaned under the strain.

At the same time, the Spoon-o-Matic roared to life and its robotic arms whirled like a pinwheel. But the bolts attaching the arms had been loosened, and a barrage of spoons sailed forth in random flurry, assaulting the unsuspecting citizens and tearing holes in the tent's fabric.

Terror took centre stage. Typically poised and polite Nod's Limbsians scrambled for the exits, tripping over one another and slipping on mustard and funnel cake frosting. Dozens of abandoned balloons drifted too close to the floodlights and popped, punctuating the chorus of screams.

"*Ladies and gentlemen!*" Benedict's ringmaster tenor rang over the loudspeaker. *"Do not panic!!"*

"Run for your lives!" shouted Marvin Matterhorn.

"Children and bakers first!" cried Buffy of Buffy's Muffins.

Edgar and Ellen watched the mayhem unfold around them.

"Brother, I'm all for a good prank," Ellen said. "But this is open warfare."

Suddenly Edgar seized Ellen's wrist.

"Ormond!" he cried. "Ormond is still in the tank! We've got to help him!"

KER-BOOOOOM!

A second blast rang through the tent, but this time it was a man who flew out of the cannon.

A smiling man.

"RONAN!" Benedict shouted. "I BEG OF YOU!"

But the caretaker had already landed midway up the pole where the break had occurred. The mast shook with his weight, and he wrapped his burly arms about it.

"He's bringing down the big top!" shouted Pollyanna. The other circus performers redoubled their efforts to usher the audience members outside to safety.

Mayor Knightleigh stumbled ahead of his terrified flock of citizens towards the exit. Mayor Blodgett and a photographer from the *Smelterburg Herald* tripped along a few steps behind.

"Knightleigh!" shouted Blodgett. "If I wanted cutlery thrown at me, I would have spent the weekend with my mother-in-law!" An errant spoon ricocheted off the visiting mayor's forehead and sent him reeling.

"I assure you," declared Knightleigh, looking back over his shoulder at Ronan. "The guilty parties shall suffer my mayoral wrath." A soup ladle smacked Mayor Knightleigh's large rump. "Eee-yow!"

Edgar and Ellen had reached the eerily motionless tank of syrup in the centre ring.

"Not even Houdini could hold his breath that long!" said Edgar.

"We need to get out!" Ellen shouted, pointing upwards. "It's all coming down!"

The circle of support posts leaned at dangerously sharp

angles while the racks of floodlights flickered on and off. Swathes of canvas dipped to the ground, blocking the exits.

"Ormond—"

Before he could take another step, Edgar found himself lifted off the ground. Manny held him and Ellen in the vice-like grips of his massive hands.

"We need to save Ormond!" Edgar wriggled in the giant's grasp as Manny carried the two to safety. "Put me down!"

Manny dropped the twins in the dirt outside the big top.

"STAY. I WILL RESCUE HIM." Manny turned to go back inside, but he was too late.

Everyone heard the final, grotesque crack of the centre pole. Supporting planks splintered like twigs, thick tent ropes ripped their stakes from the ground and went sailing into the collapsing mass of canvas. The tent puffed for a moment like a parachute, then deflated.

"Ormond!" screamed Edgar, pulling Manny's tree trunk leg. "We've got to save him!"

The Colossus bowed his gigantic head. "IT IS TOO LATE FOR ORMOND."

Dahlia, her emerald dress torn, her eyes welling with tears, sank to her knees before the rubble. "Ronan . . ."

"Ronan!" Ellen seethed. "*Ronan?*"

Suddenly from beneath the wreckage, a dust–covered figure staggered forth.

"Ormond?" Edgar peeped.

But it was not the escape artist. Circus folk and townspeople backed away. Only Dahlia raced to Ronan, when she saw what the battered caretaker dragged behind him.

The limp body of Benedict.

Ronan pulled the ringmaster out into the clearing by an ankle. Benedict's peg leg – the odd appendage that sometimes boasted playful sheaths like a unicycle, a pogo stick, and a spring–loaded chicken leg – was gone. The ivory whalebone stump had been wrenched from its socket.

The caretaker let go of Benedict's ankle, heaved a sigh, and fell to the ground like a mighty oak.

Pollyanna of the Puppets dropped to her knees and put an ear to Benedict's chest as the circus family nervously gathered around them. Finally, she lifted her head.

"Our patriarch is unconscious, but he lives! Bring me water and bandages!"

The clowns raced off to a nearby tent with impressive speed, despite their gigantic shoes, to retrieve first aid supplies.

Dahlia knelt beside the exhausted and badly bruised

Ronan. She helped the caretaker to a sitting position as Manny and a pair of mimes approached.

"OFFICER JIBBERS," Manny announced, refusing to look at Ronan or Dahlia. "ARREST THAT MAN."

A bully mime waddled up, swinging an imaginary billy club, and clapped a pair of handcuffs on Heimertz as he sat slumped in the dirt. While mimes are normally masters of the pretend, the cuffs that Officer Jibbers used to detain Heimertz were most certainly real.

"Manuel," Dahlia sobbed. "Is not right . . ."

"What about that one?" demanded Pollyanna, pointing at Dahlia. "She has aided Ronan from the beginning – I caught her *red-handed* earlier today." She grabbed Dahlia's chin and forced the botanist to look her in the face. "I threatened to tell Benedict of your treachery, so you planned this attack on our family. A fine way to repay those who took you in off the street! Officer Jabbers, arrest this woman!"

"No!" cried Dahlia, as the second mime clicked the heavy metal cuffs on her wrists.

For the first time ever, as far as the twins knew, the smile on Ronan's face quivered. Like melting snow sliding off a steep roof, the corners of his mouth slipped: down, down, down his lips fell, flopping in the shape of a sad and baggy frown.

38. Circle of Fiends

Edgar and Ellen raced after Manny, determined to help the giant recover Ormond's body – or at least the trunk that had sealed his syrupy doom.

Ellen shook her head in disbelief. "This can't be happening—"

"He's the Impossible, Ellen," Edgar said desperately. "There's still a chance . . ." He ran full force into Imogen, who blocked the twins' path.

"You . . ." Imogen said, her voice shaking, her eyes lined with tears. "How could you?"

"You did this," Gonzalo said coldly. "You destroyed the tent."

"Are you insane?" Edgar shrieked. "Ronan—"

"Ronan had accomplices!" said Merrik. "You ambushed the acrobats—"

"Distracting everyone while Ronan rigged the cannon!" Mab finished.

"You could have killed the Hei-Flyers," said Imogen.

"You're all crazy!" retorted Ellen.

"*Us* crazy? You're the ones in cahoots with that madman!" Imogen cried.

"Never," said Ellen, clenching her fists. "We've been trying to get away from him! To join you!"

"*Join* us? JOIN US? Look around! Look what you've done!"

"Ellen," Edgar said softly, "they don't know we *saved* the circus from Benedict's and Ronan's greed."

"Imogen . . ." Ellen said, meeting the eyes of each of the Irregulars. "All of you. You don't understand. We're—"

"Traitors!" the group shouted.

"Please . . ." Ellen begged. "Listen to us. We tried to save—"

"Save your stinky breath." Gonzalo tossed a frayed rope at the twins' feet. "The lasso I gave you, *Miss* Ellen. I found it tied to the cannon."

"I didn't do it! We were under the bleachers—"

"Strange place to watch a circus," Gonzalo huffed.

"We invited you into our circle," Imogen said. "We shared our secrets, our trust . . ."

"Our flants," said Phoebe.

Edgar avoided the little girl's eyes.

"Can I have my flants back now?"

"Well," Edgar fidgeted and stared at the ground. "See, Phoebe. Here's the odd thing. When we broke into the puppet house – no, wait – that didn't come out right—"

"*You* were the ones who wrecked the Marionette House!" shouted Mab.

"Puppet butchers!" Merrik yelled. "Is nothing sacred to you?"

"Where are my flants, Edgar? Did you lose them?" Phoebe asked, her eyes filling with tears. "You did, you lost them!" The tiny girl ran off sobbing.

Imogen stood nose to nose with Ellen. "You are going in the dunk tank . . . and you aren't coming out."

"Enough." Ellen rolled up her sleeves. "I tried to be nice . . . tried to tell the truth . . . but now . . ."

"Sister . . ." Edgar tugged one of Ellen's pigtails. "Time to go."

"Back off, Brother. I'm sick of—"

"Ellen! We've got company!"

Edgar swivelled his sibling's head with both hands toward Jens and Taryn Heimertz, who stalked towards them, flanked by Officers Jibbers and Jabbers.

The twins shoved past the Irregulars in a panic.

"Edgar!" Ellen tripped over a cart of flavoured ice, but Edgar dragged her along. "What do we do? Where do we go?"

"Just run!"

The mimes gained on them, swirling their imaginary clubs overhead and blowing invisible whistles.

But suddenly they stopped.

Every clown, every freak, every barker, every triple-jointed contortionist — the entire family knelt on the dusty ground in grave silence.

The twins immediately saw why.

His gargantuan arms bulging from the strain, Manny the Colossus pushed the escape artist's dented and syrup-covered steamer trunk from the rubble. Even at a fair distance, Edgar could see well enough to know the horrible truth.

Not a lock on the trunk had been opened, not a chain loosened. And not a soul in this world, no matter his lung capacity, could have endured so long inside.

Not even the Impossible.

"Ellen . . ." Edgar bowed his head.

"I know . . ." Ellen put an arm around her brother's shoulder. Then the twins turned their backs on the tragic scene: the fallen friend, the big top carnage, and the circus family they had hoped so hard to join.

Before their pursuers could resume the chase, Edgar and Ellen ran for the protective cover of the Black Tree Forest.

39. Send out the Clowns

Pollyanna of the Puppets yanked madly on the chains that bound the escape artist's trunk, her hands slipping on syrupy residue.

"Manny! Hector!" the woman cried. "Somebody help me!"

The Colossus hung his giant head. "IT IS DONE. RONAN THE MAD HAS BROUGHT DEATH UPON US."

"But we can't just leave him in there, Manny!"

One of Ormond's sequinned assistants approached the trunk with a tattered cape. She respectfully draped the cloak across the top, tears falling from her eyes.

"Yes. We are bound to leave the trunk forever sealed," the assistant said sadly. "This was our vow should Ormond ever fail to escape. It shall be his coffin."

"That was his wish," said Hector the Dissector, placing a sliced butterfly atop the cloak. "He did not want us to hack through the chains, to hammer the locks to pieces – only to find him lifeless within . . . devoid of magic and mystery . . ."

"LET US HONOUR HIM," Manny finished.

"*Dishonour!*" shouted Mayor Knightleigh, marching through the crowd. Behind him came Bob the intern, Mayor Blodgett, the *Smelterburg Herald* photographer, and several distraught Nod's Limbs citizens. "Dishonour! Disgrace!" The mayor pointed a fat finger at the severed butterfly. "Dismemberment!"

The cluster of angry Nod's Limbsians stirred behind him. Bandaged, bruised, and holding overstuffed tummies, they shouted things like "Unheard-of civic dangers!" and "Bad influence on our children!" and "Too much fat in that fudge!"

"Your abominable excuse for a community is hereby banished forthwith from the town of Nod's Limbs!" Mayor Knightleigh said to the clicking of a camera. "I give you until sunrise to have every last scrap of this circus rubbish removed from my environs!"

"Hear, hear!" hollered his citizens, rallying behind their mayor.

Mayor Blodgett, a cup of melting mango ice pressed to a bump on his forehead, encouraged the photographer to snap pictures of the big top wreckage, the escape artist's syrupy sarcophagus, and the town's raucous outburst.

Pollyanna the Puppeteer howled. "Have you no heart? One of our family has fallen!"

"I wonder what the neighbouring towns will say when they read about this," snickered Mayor Blodgett. "'Nod's Limbs: A Lovely Place to Get Crushed by Circus Freaks.' Is that too long a headline?"

Mayor Knightleigh gasped. "You wouldn't dare, Blodgett!"

The visiting mayor and his photographer quickly turned to go. "Keep up the great mayoring, Knightleigh! Soon everyone from Whistler's Glen to Snuggler's Cove will know to *stay away from Nod's Limbs*!"

Knightleigh turned to the silent circus folk. "By sunrise."

"ONE HEIMERTZ SHALL STAY BEHIND," Manny said to the mayor. "WE HAVE FAMILY BUSINESS WITH THE HOUSE . . ."

Stephanie appeared next to her father, giving him a nudge and a wink. Then she unfurled a yellowed piece of paper in front of Manny's widening eyes.

"I assure you that the house is no longer your concern," she said. "Your family business has become *our* family business. Right, Daddy?"

Manny sputtered. "HOW DID YOU GET THAT? THAT IS OURS . . ."

"Not any more. It's 'ours' now — quite legally, wouldn't you agree?" said Mayor Knightleigh, clapping a hand on his daughter's shoulder. "If *any* of your kind remain at dawn, by Nod, I will have the entire lot of you misfits hunted down and thrown into jail."

Mayor Knightleigh could see the surprised faces of the townspeople standing nearby. He had delivered a good tongue-lashing perhaps, but the mention of prison terms seemed to ruffle the faithful voters around him. The mayor gave them his best smile.

"Err . . . jail in Smelterburg, of course. They have lots of jail cells there . . . lots of criminals. They should change the town name to 'Smelterburglar.' Only one cell here in Nod's Limbs! Really more of a tourist attraction than anything else . . ."

As Mayor Knightleigh strode away with his daughter, Manny boomed, "WE'LL BE BACK, KNIGHTLEIGH. THIS ISN'T OVER."

But for the mayor and his citizens, it appeared to be. The crowds dispersed and wandered back to their homes.

"Did that man really die in that box, Daddy?" asked Timmy Poshi.

"No, no, son," Mr Poshi said weakly. "It's part of the act. He pops out safe and syrupy sound when the circus arrives at the next town."

"Oh, that's neat!"

The circus family huddled together around the coffin of Ormond the Impossible.

Hector the Dissector cupped the pieces of the butterfly atop the sealed trunk. When he opened his hands seconds later, the colourful insect fluttered up into the night sky.

The Colossus lifted up little Phoebe and placed her on

his massive shoulders. The tearful girl hugged his neck. "WE SHALL MAKE MERRY AGAIN. NOW, COME. THERE IS MUCH TO DO."

40. Small Talk

The twins watched from the forest as teams of woeful circus performers solemnly closed down tents, carts, and kiosks. Every booth on the midway folded as flat as a pizza box, as bearded ladies and tattooed men transported the entire circus universe onto rickety caravans and rusty trailers.

With Officers Jibbers and Jabbers preoccupied packing up their invisible stairs, escalators, and elevators, Edgar and Ellen left the safety of the forest to risk a closer look at Ormond's coffin and a chance to eavesdrop on the circus' plans. They tiptoed behind a wagon at the back of the caravan. One side bore a painting of two enraged gorillas tearing trees from the ground; the other three sides were barred. Carved in a wooden arch overhead were the words:

BEHOLD THE MOST DESPICABLE
CREATIONS IN ALL OF NATURE
(IF YOU CAN STOMACH THEIR AWFUL VISAGE!)

"It looks like it's over," said Ellen, peering around from behind the wagon's wheel. "They aren't even opening the box."

Edgar stifled an agonized moan. "Such a great man. Such a tragedy. And he was our only way into the circus . . ."

"Silly, silly children," said a voice from inside the wagon. The startled twins took a closer look between the bars. Hidden in shadows at the back sat Madame Dahlia and Ronan Heimertz, bound in chains. Heimertz's shackles were triple what Dahlia wore, and his chest and arms strained against them. But, though he was clamped in heavy manacles, he appeared more burdened with his own sadness than with his chains.

"Well, well," said Ellen. "You two certainly got what you deserved."

Dahlia sighed. "You have been fooled – the whole circus has been fooled. Fooled by a master deceiver."

"The only deceivers here are you two!" said Edgar.

"Oh? Why would Ronan shoot himself up to pole? It was already breaking! He held pole together to let others escape. He saved our lives."

"A likely story—"

"Dirty work you have done for dirty man who could not risk it himself . . ." Dahlia rattled her chains. " . . . who was not *capable* of it himself."

"Come on, Ellen," Edgar said. "We've wasted enough time with these conspirators."

Suddenly Heimertz sprang. A chain on one wrist snapped as he reached a powerful arm through the bars, grabbing Edgar by his pyjamas and pulling him close. The boy went stiff.

But Heimertz did not crush Edgar; he did not break him in two. Instead, for the first time in all the years the twins had known him, Heimertz spoke.

"Pet . . ." His voice was dusty and deep, like a boulder rolling in front of a tomb. With his free hand he reached into a pocket of his overalls and pulled out a small, white object, which he placed in Edgar's palm. ". . . is dying."

"A s-seed?" stammered Edgar.

"It's one of Morella's seeds," said Ellen quietly. "Her *tooth-like* seeds."

"Morella?" said Edgar. "Oh no . . . the *bite*."

Heimertz pointed to the eyeball poking out of Edgar's satchel. "I have failed. You must dig out the spring. Save Pet."

He released Edgar, and the wheels of the prison creaked and began to roll forwards as the caravan pulled away.

"*Us* save Pet? Isn't that the kind of thing your family should do?" asked Ellen.

"It is Heimertz family's vow to protect balm, not one-eyed creatures," said Dahlia. "Remember mad duke? Balm, in wrong hands, leads to destruction. The spring here, it is sealed by fallen rock, sealed by Fate. The family will not open it, even if it means *ithune* must die."

The twins watched helplessly as the gorilla cage lurched away with the sad procession. Manny and the clowns held aloft Ormond's trunk, and the caravan rolled past the Waxworks and out of Nod's Limbs.

41. Now You Syrup, Now You Don't

Edgar and Ellen sat in the twilit grounds of the Waxworks, shivering. The last wagon had disappeared over the horizon, and the stars in the east were fading to make way for the sun.

Edgar gently pulled Pet from his satchel. It barely blinked; its eye was now completely coated in a thick, grey film.

"Could Pet *really* be dying, Ellen?"

"We knew Morella's seeds were the antidote to Pet's tears. We should have guessed that they're also the antidote to *Pet*." Ellen stroked the creature's hair.

"Don't be so quick to believe our old caretaker. Remember the tongs? The torture?"

"Edgar, don't you see? He was *extracting* the seed! It was still in Pet. Poisoning it – but why would Heimertz risk banishment from his family to save Pet?"

Pet rustled on the ground, and the twins saw that it was painstakingly writing in the dirt.

"Ah, twins . . . you could not see . . . until the end,
He risked it all . . . because he was my friend."

Edgar looked up at Ellen. "All this . . . for a friend . . ."

He stopped abruptly as a twig cracked in the forest behind them.

"Shh."

Crack.

"Somebody's on to us, Ellen."

The rustling of leaves and the snapping of branches grew louder, but then diminished as whatever it was moved on.

"What's that smell?" asked Edgar. "It's almost like . . . like . . ."

"Maple syrup!" gasped Ellen.

The twins scrambled into the brush to find a trail of broken branches. Further on they saw a clearing of matted pine needles, as if someone had been sitting there for some time. The waning moonlight beamed just enough through a gap in the treetops for the twins to see some very familiar objects: a straitjacket with hidden breakaway stitching, six imitation Stock Maiden locks with spring-release buttons, and a pair of Jestofer handcuffs that felt suspiciously lighter than the ones Edgar had escaped from in Ormond's tent.

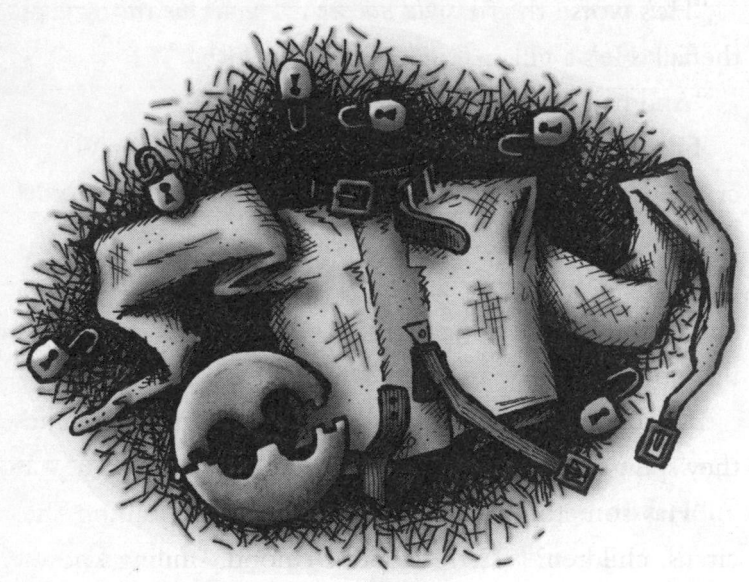

"Hey, these props are *fake!*" Edgar threw the cuffs to the ground.

"*Ormond escaped. He's alive,*" said Ellen. In her hands she held Benedict's whalebone leg. Impressed into the ivory peg were the three ambers — the spider, the cricket, the dragonfly — three keys that, when pressed into their special sockets, unlocked a small safe built into the hollow appendage. A tiny door hung open, revealing an empty compartment within. "And now he's got whatever Benedict hid in here."

"I can't believe it, Ellen. Ormond's a phoney? A sham?"

"He's worse than a sham, Edgar. He set us up to take the fall. He's a villain."

"And he's getting away!"

The twins sped along a well-marked trail. When crushed pine needles and bent branches couldn't guide their way, globs of syrup did.

They ran until they emerged from the forest onto the rails of the old train line that ran into town. They looked up and down the tracks, but saw nothing.

But then someone cleared his throat behind them, and they spun around.

"Has something dashed your dreams of joining the circus, children?" There stood Ormond, smiling knowingly.

Edgar trembled. "Dreams dashed? You better believe it – just like your plan to . . . to do whatever you're about to do, faker!"

"My plan?" scoffed Ormond. "My only plan is to relish my first fresh breaths of freedom. The gruelling life of the circus is in my past, as are you two."

The twins took a step towards him and he pulled a thick club from his robes.

"Stop where you are," he said. "I've already used this once tonight."

"On Benedict," said Ellen.

"He would hardly have sat still to let me open his most private safe, would he?"

"What did you take? What was worth all this trouble?" asked Edgar.

"A trifle, really. A mere scrap of paper. But I was fortunate to find the right buyer. A rich buyer."

"Was it evidence that incriminated Heimertz?" asked Ellen. "Have you been working this hard for some kind of revenge?"

"Ronan? You poor, confused sparrows. Who cares about that oaf? His love of the *ithune* has clearly clouded his brain – digging out a sacred spring to save the creature – what nonsense. He was well on his way to getting replaced here no matter what I did. When that soft-hearted idiot threw himself against the pole . . . *ha!* . . . he just dug his own grave deeper."

"Stealing that lasso? You set us up to take the fall," said Ellen.

"Set you up?" Ormond asked, with some confusion. "Ah, I see. That must have been my accomplice. Impressive work – really taking care to misdirect the audience."

"An accomplice?" said Edgar. "Of course you had help. Who?"

"Did I say accomplice?" asked Ormond. "I meant . . . *apprentice*. You'll meet her soon enough, I wager."

Ormond tucked the club away. "I tire of this – you are delaying the beginning of my luxurious retirement in some faraway paradise. I must now take my leave."

He whipped off his hat and pulled out a small cloth bag.

"Remember, poppets. Life is naught but smoke and mirrors." He flipped the hat atop his head, then smashed the bag onto the ground. A silvery cloud filled the air, and the twins coughed and sputtered. When the acrid fog cleared and the twins could breathe again, Ormond was gone.

42. Unwelcome Home

The twins trudged south towards their house with heads hung low. Edgar muttered over and over, "*Betrayed. Betrayed. Betrayed.*"

Ellen pulled out Pet again and cradled the creature in her arms. "We have to get some balm or Pet's a goner."

"*Betray*— what? Oh, balm. You're forgetting the explosion. We destroyed what was left."

"There's more, Edgar. Lots more. Underground."

"Not even Heimertz could dig it out, Ellen."

Ellen stopped and turned to her brother. "What choice do we have now? We're too late to rescue Heimertz, too late to foil Ormond—"

"But not too late to save Pet."

"Not yet."

Covered in dirt and grime, Edgar and Ellen trekked back to their house. Every so often they'd look to the road out of town for a sign that the circus had returned, that someone had seen through Ormond's deceit. But the caravans were long gone, and all that remained was a pile of broken beams and scraps of torn canvas flapping in the breeze.

The path we took has only spawned
A trail, a swathe of broken bonds,

And we, who never could be conned,
Fell victim to that snake, Ormond!
Was it folly to pursue
A voyage out and life anew?
Naive and blind to what was true,
Alone again once more, we two.
Still, with one last blow we're met:
Without the balm, what hope for Pet?

"And we'll never know what Ormond stole from Benedict's leg, will we, Sister?"

"Or what he got in return," Ellen added. "Whatever he took, it sounds incredibly valuable."

The twins had just turned down the nameless lane that led to their house when they saw a limousine idling before their door.

They ran the final stretch, but Stephanie Knightleigh was already skipping back to the car with a hammer in her hand. She saw Edgar and Ellen and smiled as she waved a crusty, yellowed document in the air, the same document she had flashed in Manny's face mere hours earlier. And, not too much earlier than that, the prized document that had come at so serious a price for Benedict.

"Smoke and mirrors, little poppets!" the curly-haired girl taunted, hopping into the car. The limo zoomed down the rocky driveway, turning on to Ricketts Road with a screech of rubber.

The twins stared blankly at the front of the door, where a bright red piece of paper had been nailed:

EVICTION NOTICE

By the power invested in me (by the deed to this property, recently purchased from one Ormond Heimertz), I hereby demand the immediate evacuation of these premises by all people, animals, pests, and bothersome twins.

DEMOLITION TO BEGIN FORTHWITH.

Yours truly,

Mayor Knightleigh

(P.S. Vote Knightleigh!)

Edgar & Ellen

NOD'S LIMBS

It's all-out war with the Knightleigh family, and Edgar and Ellen are losing ground. But everyone's attention is diverted by the ghostly hand of fortune: Augustus Nod has launched a treasure hunt from beyond the grave! The twins must solve the riddles and discover Nod's lost golden limbs before the Knightleighs bury the past – and the twins with it!

Coming Soon!